Let

(McClain Brothers: Book 3)

Alexandria House

Pink Cashmere Publishing, LLC
Arkansas, USA

ISBN: 9781729208540

Printed in the United States of America

First Printing 2018

Pink Cashmere Publishing, LLC
pinkcashmerepub@gmail.com

Let Me Show You

Nolan McClain is the smart one, the driven one, the one who goes for what he wants, meticulously plans his steps, and thinks he has his life all mapped out...until he lays eyes on Bridgette Turner.

Bridgette Turner is just as driven and focused as Nolan, but when her past comes back to haunt her, she finds herself knocked off balance and all her hard work in jeopardy.

What Nolan feels for her is real, but Bridgette is skeptical. Will she let him show her his heart?

To my readers, thank you from the bottom of my heart.

A special thank you to Sharon Blount and the members of the Building Relationships Around Books Online Book Club.

1

Nolan

Her ambition was one of the first things I noticed about her. That, and the fact that she knew how to work a room.

Like me.

We often ran in the same social circles because she was my sister-in-law, Jo's, assistant and friend, but those titles weren't the beginning and end of her. She was also an actress, a talented one. She was…remarkable.

What attracted me to her initially was our similarities, our comparable drive and desire to succeed. It didn't hurt that she was gorgeous in a girl-next-door kind of way—flawless copper-colored skin, cute little pouty lips, big expressive eyes. She was taller than me in heels, but shit, I actually kind of liked that. Thin, with just enough curves and a great ass. Always put together, always *on*, as if she knew opportunity might knock at any moment and she wasn't about to miss out. She spoke her mind and laughed out loud. She was…she was perfect, but I froze up around her, couldn't get my thoughts to align with my words, ended up bringing up something trivial or benign when I tried to have a conversation with her, and that was out of character for me. I was a talker, had always been smooth with it, too. I can't lie; Bridgette Turner intimidated the shit out of me, but I was going to have to get myself together since I couldn't shake what I was feeling for her. I'd tried, but just couldn't.

The main issue was that I hadn't really had to try when it came to women in a long time. I just pointed, and the women were handed to me thanks to my membership in the very exclusive *Gallery*, a place that specialized in fulfilling the needs of any man who could afford to pay the club's fees. I could pay, and had enjoyed the benefits of that affiliation for years, but now? Well, now I was feeling far less than fulfilled. Now I had a thing for Bridgette Turner.

Now, I only wanted her.

"Mm, you vant make sex again?" Galina's voice was husky, heavily Russian-accented, and drowsy as she scooted closer to me in bed, resting her hand on my Bridgette-induced erection. Yeah, just thinking about her did that to me.

Before I could answer her, she was sliding down my body, ducking beneath the covers. So I rested my head on the pillow and closed my eyes, imagining that she was Bridgette.

Bridgette

"Jessie Mae? That you?"

I took the phone from my ear and stared at the screen. My iPhone had informed me that the call came from Alabama, which was why I answered it. I thought it was my friend, Karen, with another update. She was how I kept up with everyone back home without interacting with them. I knew her number but thought maybe she had a new one or something. However, this wasn't Karen. This voice...I knew it well, and with it came an avalanche of dark memories, memories that made my hands shake and shit, and I wasn't the nervous type. I considered myself rather fearless. But this voice? It reduced me to a scared child, a state I absolutely despised to be in. So it was obvious that I needed to hang up, but I couldn't, because despite the darkness and pain the owner of the voice had allowed to compose my childhood remembrances, despite the years it shaved off my maturity, I kind of missed hearing it. So instead of ending the call, I activated the speakerphone and closed my eyes as she repeated herself.

"Jessie Mae?"

I hadn't heard or seen that name in a long time, not since I legally changed it. I'd gone by Bridgette since middle school, but my high school diploma still said Jessie Mae Turner.

I wondered if there was a way to change it.

Because I hated that damn name and the bitch it honored.

The only reason I didn't change my last name was because I actually liked my father.

She said the name once more, mumbled something I couldn't decipher, and then she hung up.

I stood there for a moment staring at my phone before tucking it in my pocket, inspecting myself in the restroom mirror, and leaving the sleek office building. I'd killed the audition I'd just finished, but then again, I always did. As I slid behind the steering wheel of my Kia, I threaded my fingers through my freshly-relaxed hair, squeezed my eyes shut, and prayed I'd get the part, because acting was the great equalizer for me. It reduced the amount of Jessie Mae Turner left in my soul. And I needed that more than anything.

2

Bridgette

"...I think that's all I had on our agenda for today. Oh, wait...I rescheduled your maternity photo shoot for this weekend like you asked," I said, my eyes glued to the agenda on my iPad.

Jo finished chewing the rest of her apple and rubbed her humongous belly. "Good! I'm so glad we got that worked out since Everett couldn't reschedule his appearance on that show. He tried to back out, but I wouldn't let him. His fans would've had a fit."

"Yeah, I know. Folks love them some Big South, and he's talking about retiring, too? That might be one of his last shows."

She shook her head as she popped a grape into her mouth. I swear this baby made her eat all damn day! "Girl, please. The way he stays in the studio, he ain't retiring from nothing. He'll probably just do shorter tours or something."

"I don't know, Jo. He really hates leaving you, and it'll be hard to tour with two kids."

She shrugged as she grabbed a banana from a bowl on the coffee table in front of us. "We'll see."

"Yeah."

"So, how was your audition from earlier today?" Jo garbled through a mouth full of banana.

"It—"

Her doorbell cut me off, and then she just sat there and looked at me.

Rolling my eyes, I said, "I'll get it."

She swallowed her food, gave me a huge grin, and said, "Thanks, Bridge."

I rolled my eyes again, and mumbled, "Lazy, pregnant, always-eating ass…"

"Uh, I heard that!" she yelled at my back.

"Good!" I replied, as I made it to the door and checked the peephole, knowing whoever it was had already been cleared by Chink, their bodyguard who was manning the gate that day. I guess it was just a habit since I still lived out in the regular world where you had to fend for yourself.

Seeing that it was Nolan, with his fine ass—all the McClain brothers were fine, by the way; even Neil with his tortured self—I opened the door and smiled at him. Nolan was a nice guy if a little artless at times. I liked him.

"Hi," he said, returning my smile.

"Hey, Nolan. Come on in."

Stepping over the threshold and into the foyer holding a leather satchel, his eyes never left me. If I didn't know he had a thing for clear women, I'd almost think—

"Hi," he repeated, still smiling.

I took him in, all of him—smooth toasted brown skin, neat mustache and goatee framing his full lips, thick eyebrows, eyelashes I'd pay good money to have glued to mine, piercing dark eyes, and hair in a precise Caesar cut. He was in his usual attire—buttoned up but not quite formal. His style was that of a relaxed businessman—usually rocking a suit with no tie—well-groomed, expensive-looking, and he always smelled divine. He was about an inch taller than me, and I could tell there was a nice body under his clothes. If Nolan McClain liked black women, I would've gladly rocked his whole world, because everything about him turned me on. He ticked off all the boxes for my prototype of the perfect man.

"Hey," I said. This entire exchange was awkward as hell, though. You'd think he didn't know how to interact with a woman, but I'd seen him talk to his sister, Jo, and Leland's wife, Kim, plus his harem of comrades plenty of times, and he never seemed this odd.

He was actually pretty articulate and very intelligent. Maybe it was me…

"Who is it—oh, hey, Nolan! You looking for Everett?" Jo's voice echoed in the foyer.

"Uh, yeah. He here?" he responded, still looking at me. Almost in a flirty way. But…nah.

"Mm-hmm. He's in his office."

"Uh, thanks. See you ladies later," he said, giving me another smile before heading down the hall.

I lifted a brow and stared down at my short friend. "How you gonna have me answer the door then waddle your ass in here anyway?"

She shrugged. "I wanted to see who it was."

"I swear I don't know why I deal with you."

"Because you love me, and I pay you well."

"The second part is true."

"Hateful heifer. Come on and take me to get a burger. Then we can pick Nat up from daycare, and on the way, you can finally tell me what you and Nolan were talking about at Leland's and Kim's party last week."

"There's nothing to tell. He was asking me about that new Michael B. Jordan movie. He wanted to know if I've seen it and what I thought about it."

"That's it?"

"Yeah. What'd you think we were talking about?"

"I don't know, but you looked irritated. I thought maybe he was hitting on you or something."

"Would you quit that? How was he gonna be hitting on me when his *Red Sparrow* was a few feet away from us?"

"Because he likes you. How many times I gotta tell you that?"

"He likes pastry, *not* sweet potato pie. Croissants, *not* cornbread. Kale, *not* collard greens. Ham and cheese, *not* ham hocks. Mayonnaise *not* sandwich spread. You really need to stop playing with my emotions, anyway, bad as I want me a McClain brother, knowing you and your sister-in-law got the only two viable ones."

"Nope. He likes you *and* he's your type."

As I stated before, he really *was* my type, but I wasn't going to admit it. "So, he's supposed to like me because Leland told South he saw him looking at my booty? He was probably trying to figure out if this out-of-control thing is real. I really have got to do something about my ass. I mean, I know I look good, and in any other career, it'd be an asset, but I'm an actress, a fucking thespian, not an Instagram model! It doesn't go with my body at all…"

"I'll trade you your ass for my stomach."

"Hell no. You can keep that. It looks like you're having triplets."

"I knoooooow. Damn those Big South genes!"

"That baby prolly gonna come out six-four with a goatee and some bass in his—or her—voice."

"Shut up, hooker," she groaned, as she rubbed her stomach again. "Back to the issue at hand: why were you looking so crazy when Nolan was talking to you at the party, then?"

"I don't know. Tommy was there, and I had gotten used to not seeing him since he moved to St. Louis. It just felt…weird."

"You miss him?"

"I miss his penis."

"Bridgette!"

"What? You asked. Wait, was that your stomach growling? Out loud?"

She nodded. "Yeah, I'm starving."

"You've been eating since I got here!"

"Don't you think I know that? Come on, let's go get this burger and then hurry back because I need to attack Everett after I eat. I am so horny right now."

"Shit, I bet you are. Look, you're gonna have to start paying me extra for these food runs, and you know good and well you can't leave without security. You ain't gonna have Big South jumping on me."

"Ugh! Let me text Oba so he can drive us."

"And you're buying me a shake."

"Them shakes are responsible for that ass Nolan is so fond of."

"You really need to quit," I sighed, as I followed her out the front door.

Nolan

"So we're actually doing this? We're casting Honey Combs as the lead? Shit." Everett shook his head as he stared down at the paperwork I'd brought with me.

"It's smart business, Ev. She's a star with a huge fan base. That's guaranteed ticket sales and a selling point for negotiating a distribution deal. And did you look at her reels?"

He dragged his hand down his face. "Yeah. She can act. Shocked the hell outta me considering she can't sing for shit. All she does is whisper in the microphone. Her fans are crazy."

"Yeah, her voice is trash, but shit, she ain't gotta sing in the movie. Her momager said she's specifically looking for parts with no singing involved."

"Probably because her ass knows she can't sing."

"Hell, she's got to know."

"What you offer her?"

"Turn the page."

He did, then looked up at me. "For real? And she accepted it? How the fuck you get her management to agree to this?"

I shrugged. "You know me. I get shit done."

"What you promise, Nole?"

"Uh, I had to guarantee roles for her sisters."

"Shit. Can they even act?"

"I have no idea."

"Nole, man…"

"No, listen…Jazz, Honey's character, has three sisters, right?

Candy and Sugar are gonna play two of her sisters."

He sighed. "At least they're small roles. One of the sisters doesn't even speak through the whole movie."

"Ev, do I look stupid? I wasn't giving all three of them big roles and letting them screw them up. The name of the movie is *Floetic Lustice,* not Confection. I ain't letting them take over this thing."

"You talk to Adams? He on board with Honey playing his love interest?"

I nodded as I reclined in my chair. "I thought it was gonna be a hard sell, because you know he wanted a dark-skinned chick to play Jazz, but as it turns out, he was good with it. Said his wife would be more comfortable with someone like Honey."

"Yeah, Honey is the polar opposite of his wife. You seen her? Tall, dark, real pretty."

"Of course I have. She signed on to do wardrobe, remember?"

"Yeah, yeah. So, Mr. Casting Director, have you found someone to play Cynthia, Jazz's BFF?"

"Uh, yeah. That's a huge role, and we need an experienced actress to fill it, so I was thinking Jo's friend, Bridgette, would be perfect for it."

"Word?"

"Yeah. Don't you think so?"

"Yeah, but I didn't know you'd seen her in action. Did she submit her reels or something?"

"Naw, I checked out that movie she was in that you produced. She really stood out."

"Oh, a'ight. You gonna just...offer the role to her unsolicited?"

"I was thinking maybe you could..."

Everett just sat there and stared at me.

"What? You don't wanna offer it to her? You think she's wrong for it?" I asked.

"Naw, I think she'd be great, and I'm cool with offering her the part. I'll contact her agent, but you know...it'd be cheaper for you to just ask her out, Nole."

"What?"

"You like her, don't you? Tell the truth. That's why you're giving her this part."

I shrugged. "No—I mean, she's a good actress, and she's-she's...cool."

He kept staring at me.

"Damn, man! Shit! Okay, I like her," I confessed. "What of it?"

Everett tilted his head to the side and stretched his eyes wide. "I don't know. Just can't believe it. It's crazy."

"How is it crazy? She's attractive and talented, got a great personality. What straight man wouldn't be interested in her?"

"One who don't like black women."

"Who said I don't like black women?"

"You always walking around with them Bulgarian chicks said it."

"They're *Russian*, Ev. How many times I gotta tell you that?"

"Shit, ain't that the same thing?"

"Really, Ev?"

He shrugged.

"Anyway, I love black women. I have my reasons for not dating them."

"But you wanna date Bridgette?"

This time, I shrugged.

"What does that mean? A shrug ain't an answer, Nolan."

"Didn't you just shrug?"

"Yeah, but I ain't the one with the MBA. Use some of them educated words you love using when you're doing business and explain this shit to me."

"I-shit, I don't know if I *can* date her."

He frowned. "What you mean?"

"I mean, every time I approach her or try to have a conversation with her, I freeze up, fumble my words, and start talking about stupid, unimportant stuff."

"Why?"

"I don't know? Out of practice, I guess."

He leaned back in his chair and shook his head. "I told your ass about that point-and-click fucking you been doing."

"And I told *your ass* I don't do online dating or whatever."

"Then how the hell you find that many Croatian chicks that like black dudes?"

"Can we get back to the subject at hand? What I'm saying is, since I don't really have to try with the women I usually date, I feel kind of awkward around her."

"Then stop feeling awkward, nigga. Bridgette is cool people. I mean, shit...black women don't attack on sight. They ain't all angry bitches like they're stereotyped to be."

"I know that."

"Then just talk to her. You the smoothest nigga I know. Hell, you almost as smooth as me, can always talk your way into or out of anything, by far the smartest McClain brother. Work your magic on her. Ain't no need in you being nervous."

"You're right, man. Thanks."

"Oh, and look, if you serious about getting with her, you gonna have to stop bringing them Slovakian motherfuckers with you everywhere you go. It's hard to shoot your shot when it looks like you already got a woman. Ain't no woman—black, white, or green—going for that shit. At least any woman worth having would have a problem with that."

I nodded. "I know. I just…"

"Don't like being alone. I know. But you gotta make sacrifices for what you want. If you really want her, and you show her that, then you won't have to be alone for long."

"You really think so? You think I have a real chance with her?" I asked.

"Nigga, you're a McClain man. Hell yeah, you got a chance! Now, let's get back to work. Who we got playing Jazz's mama?"

I shrugged again, staring down at the stack of papers before me on the edge of Everett's desk. "I was thinking Esther would work for that role."

He shot straight to his feet. "Hell. Fucking. Naw! You must be done lost your got-damn mind!"

I fell back in my chair, finally breaking character and laughing so hard that tears filled my eyes. "I'm just messing with you, big brother. Calm your big ass down!"

Everett fell back into his chair, and mumbled, "Man, don't be playing with me like that."

I couldn't stop laughing as we continued our meeting.

3

Bridgette

"Hewwo!" Jo's garbled voice boomed from my car's speakers.

"What is your always-eating-ass chewing on now that's got you sounding like Nat-Nat?"

"Some ribs." Her voice was much clearer that time, so I guessed she'd swallowed.

"Ribs at nine in the damn morning?"

"They were leftovers from last night. What are you doing?"

"Leaving the gym. Girl, I kicked my own ass today. Did like a hundred squats after doing five miles on the treadmill."

"Those squats are responsible for that donk you got. You know that, right?"

"No, the squats keep the thing firm. If I can't get rid of it, I can at least keep it from jiggling all over the place."

"Why don't you work out over here anymore? You know Everett doesn't care if you use his gym."

As I pulled off the lot and into traffic, I said, "Because, one: I haven't gotten over that time I was on the treadmill and both him and Leland came in shirtless to lift weights. I love you, Jo, but that motherfucker you married is fine, so fine I actually stumbled and almost broke my ass on that treadmill. Then there's Leland, who at the time was single but didn't pay my fine ass a second glance, and well, *he* was so fine, I had visions of making him take this coochie. And if by chance no fine McClains are present, I ain't about to be in there working out while you sit on a weight bench and watch me while stuffing your face with whatever you can find. I'm good with my *Be Fit* membership."

Her, "You're exaggerating, I don't eat that much," sounded like…shit, I don't know.

"Jo! Can you put the damn ribs down until after we have this conversation?"

Nothing from her, and then whimpering. This damn pregnancy had my BFF's emotions all over the place. She wasn't nearly this sensitive when she was carrying Nat.

"I'm sorry," she whined. "I'm just so damn hungry. And horny. All the time! All I do is eat and screw."

"I bet South is loving that."

"He iiiiiis," she sobbed.

"Okay, calm down. I didn't mean to yell. Look, I just wanted to call and thank you for getting your hubby to cast me in his movie. When my agent called and said McClain Films wanted me for their first project, I was like, 'Go best fran, that's my best fran!' And it's a huge role, too! Good looking out! We start table reads this afternoon. I am so ready!!"

She sniffled, and said, "You're thanking the wrong person. I didn't have nothing to do with that."

I frowned slightly. "Oh? Well, I already thanked South, so…"

"Wrong again. Nolan personally chose you for that role."

"He-he did?"

"Mm-hmm. I told you he likes you."

As I stared at the crawling traffic before me, I decided maybe she was right, but still said, "I guess, but it doesn't matter if he does."

"Why not?"

"You know why not."

"Just because things didn't work out with Tommy doesn't mean you and Nolan can't work out. You and Tommy weren't compatible. You said yourself y'all had nothing to talk about and only really got along when you were having sex. You and Nolan have the film industry in common if nothing else."

"I'm back to focusing on my career, Jo. I don't have time for

Nolan McClain or any other man right now. Got too much going on." *Getting strange phone calls and shit...*

"But—"

"Jo, drop it."

She sighed loudly into the phone. "I'm happy in love with a good man despite *Tea Steepers* posting one of my fresh maternity shoot pics with the caption, 'Bag Secured.' I just want you to be happy, too. You *and* Sage."

"Sage has Gavin. She's good."

"I know, but I want you to have your Gavin, or actually, your Nolan. He's really sweet and smart, you know? Handsome, and his bank account ain't hurting, either. He's like an investment guru according to Everett."

You forgot fine. "And he has a thing for Russian women."

"No, he has a thing for *you*."

"Mm-hmm. I'll talk to you later, Jo."

"Bye, Bridge. And remember, like you once told me, you deserve to live."

"I'm living, Jo."

"No, you work all the time."

"You're demanding."

"Once again, then you're fired."

"Ho', please."

"I'm just saying, when Nolan asks you out—"

"*If,* not *when.*"

"No, *when* he asks you out, please give him a chance."

"*If* that ever happens, I will, because shit, he's a McClain. He's guaranteed to have a big dick."

"How do you know that? Maybe Ev is the only McClain with a big dick."

"Naw, Nolan walks like he's carrying a heavy load down there. So do Leland and Neil. I peeped that a while back."

"Good Lord. Bye, fool."

"Bye."

Nolan

"Man, you a fool," I said through a chuckle as my boy, Lazarus, finished the story of his latest escapade. I had known him since college, and even back then, he was making claims like this. Let his ugly ass tell it, he was always getting it in. Back in the day, I was pretty sure he was lying, but now that he was a big name in Hollywood? He might've been telling the truth. I'd definitely seen him out and about with some winners.

"Nah, man! I'm for real. That thang was so good, ole girl had me hitting them 1990s Maxwell high notes. Shit, had my ass squealing like Prince in that motherfucker. I was like, 'ow-oh!' Her pussy was on fire!"

"You stupid, Laz! A damn clown!"

"I'm serious! You have no idea!"

I shook my head. "Same old Lazarus. Hey, I'm glad to have you as a part of this project, man. I know you're a big-time director now, so…"

"Nole, man, you called and I'm here. And shit, y'all paying me good."

"Not as good as Netflix did for that Kevin Hart flick you directed for them."

"Yeah, you're right, and your budget is shitty, too."

"Man, fuck you."

Lazarus threw his big-ass head back and laughed. "But seriously, you're my boy, Nole. We been friends for too many years for me not to be a part of your first film."

"'Preciate it, man."

"And, your brother is backing it, too? It's a bona fide hit with his name attached to it."

"Let's hope so."

He hopped up from his seat and extended his fist across my desk to me. As I dapped him up, he said, "Let me get to work. Wanna sit in on this table read I'm about to do with Honey Combs and Bridgette Turner?"

"I might pop in there in a minute."

Lazarus nodded and left my little office within the small McClain Films building. It was a warehouse Everett and I paid to have converted into a network of tiny offices for our abbreviated staff, a couple of spaces for filming, and a sound studio. Most of *Floetic Lustice*—the story of a popular poet and a talented female DJ falling in love—would be shot at *Second Avenue*, the club I managed. A few scenes would be filmed in my Malibu home, and we were thinking about taking the crew out of state for a few scenes that were to take place in Montana. That was a big *if*, because I was determined to stay under budget. I would cut corners any way I could, hence the filming at my house.

Filmmaking had always been a dream and a passion of mine, so much so that I'd gotten my bachelor's in filmmaking, added the MBA on because I figured it wouldn't hurt, and well, school had always been as easy for me as anything creative and abstract had always been for Neil. It was almost like we were two halves of one brain. I was the analytical one while Neil dealt more in the arts. Growing up, we complemented each other. But now? Neil just…well, I tried not to think about him too much. Him, his life, and the way he lived it could depress the shit out of me if I let it. He was my twin, and we'd been close growing up and into adulthood, but he lost his way, and there wasn't a damn thing I could do about it other than worry about him, and I was over that. I was having enough trouble keeping my own stuff straight; I didn't need to add stressing over him to my list of concerns. We barely talked anymore, and since he'd been staying with Everett, he'd been avoiding me, but it was what it was.

"Knock, knock."

My head snapped up, and my eyes instantly met hers. She was smiling as she said, "I hope I'm not bothering you. I just wanted to thank you for allowing me to be a part of this project. I'm so excited to be working with *the* Lazarus Holmes!"

"Oh, no problem. I should be thanking you for agreeing to take the role. You are very talented."

Her pretty eyes widened. "Thank you. I appreciate that."

My eyes glided over her slim body in a short skirt, a sheer blouse, and heels that looked like they put her at least three inches taller than me. *Shit*. "Yeah. You're a scene-stealer. You fill the screen."

Her smile expanded. "I didn't realize you'd seen any of my work."

"I have, and uh…I'm a fan, Ms. Turner. A *huge* fan." *Aw, shit! That was halfway smooth. I'm back!*

Bridgette rested a hand on her chest. "Call me Bridgette, and a fan? Well, Mr. McClain—"

My phone chimed, and I instinctively looked down at it to read the message previewed on the screen. "Jesse," I murmured.

"What?" Her voice sounded strained, and when I looked up from my phone, I saw that her smile had faded away, replaced by a ghosted look.

I glanced down at my phone again, trying to figure out what caused the shift in her energy. "Uh, I just got a text from the club's assistant manager. Jesse's a good employee, usually handles everything on his own when I'm not around, so for him to be texting me, I know something's up. Probably something that'll require a lot of work for me, and the club's not even open right now." I ended my statement with a chuckle, hoping that would erase the creases in her forehead.

Instead, she stared at me, or actually, she stared *through* me for a full minute before shaking her head, and saying, "Uh, I gotta go," and turning on her heels, leaving my office and leaving me confused as hell. Confused, and turned on by the view of her perfect ass as she left.

4

Bridgette

"Aw, thank you, Kim! I love it!" Jo gushed, as she peered at the gorgeous bassinette she'd just unwrapped. Leland and his wife had to have spent a lot of money for that thing. It looked like something that belonged in a palace!

This backyard baby shower was lit, full of celebrities or women married to celebrities, while their men congregated in the house. So far, Jo had received three baby strollers, the bassinette, a cradle, four car seats and tons of designer clothes—for a little girl since, as the shower organizer, it was my duty to reveal the sex to the attendees. Jo had given me the sealed results of the sex-determination ultrasound weeks earlier, and I had to damn near muzzle Sage to keep her from spilling the beans. The gifts were how the sex was revealed to Jo and South. South's big ass damn near collapsed when he saw all those pink clothes. I think he was both happy and petrified to be adding more estrogen to his household. Anyway, Jo was going to have a lot to donate to charity, which was her plan for the surplus.

My eyes perused the attendees and settled on South's sister, Kat. She was so pretty. It was a shame how her soon-to-be ex-husband did her, but she seemed happy and content holding little Leland in her lap with his juicy self. I swear, she always had that baby!

Sniffling coming from my right made me turn to see what the hell was going on with Sage. Yes, this was a beautiful occasion and we were both happy for Jo, but she'd literally been bawling since she arrived. Was her ass pregnant, too? Hell, I hoped not, because although her man was cute and seemed to really be into her, he was not the most reliable member of the male species. Dude had had four different jobs in the six months he and Sage had been together.

I handed Jo another gift. "From me and Sage," I informed her.

"Oh, okay!" She ripped into it, lifted the box holding the video baby monitor, and then grinned at me. "It's the one that hooks up to my cell phone! Thanks, ladies! I love it!"

I smiled as she pulled me into a hug. It was hard as hell to shop for her given her hubby's net worth, so I was glad she'd mentioned the monitor during one of our conversations. When she stood and walked over to Sage to give her a hug, the waterworks returned. Jo had just reclaimed her seat and I was about to pull Sage into the house to see what in the world was going on with her when my phone began to buzz in the pocket of my maxi skirt. After I checked it, I handed Jo a gift from some record executive and excused myself, hurrying into the house, checking to be sure no one was in the kitchen.

Instead of hello, I answered it with, "You gave that woman my number?!"

"Uh-um, yes," Karen stammered.

"When we made this arrangement, I told you not to give my number to anyone, especially her!" I hissed through clenched teeth. "I can't change it, because too many people in the industry have it now!"

"I know I wasn't supposed to give your number to anyone, but I thought you wouldn't mind in this case."

"In this case? What are you talking about? What on this earth could be so drastic that you'd give *her* my number?!"

"Bridgette, she's your mother. We've talked about this. At some point, you have to communicate with her again. You can't expect me to keep tabs on her for you forever."

"First of all, that motherfucker is a lot of things, but she is *not* my mother. She's not a mother to anyone! Second, if you were tired of our arrangement, the thing to do would've been for you to call me and tell me and I would've been good with it, not ambush me by giving that woman my got-damn number!"

"Okay, I need you to calm down."

"I *am* fucking calm!"

She sighed loudly into the phone. "Bridgette, look…I thought she should've been the one to tell you about her mother, *your grandmother*. Not me."

"Why? What is it? Is she dead or something?"

"Yes, Bridgette. She died of a heart attack a couple of weeks ago."

I stood there, letting my eyes survey my best friend's gorgeous kitchen; then I released a wry chuckle, and said, "Good."

"Bridgette—"

"And thank you for informing me. Thank you for…everything, but you're right. It's time for us to end this arrangement. You don't have to keep tabs on my folks anymore. It's been years. I should've let you off the hook a long time ago."

"You don't have to do this. I don't mind—"

"No, it's okay. Really, thank you."

"Okay, um…are you going to call your—are you going to call her back?"

"No," I said softly, then ended the call and stood there in the middle of the kitchen staring at my phone in my hand. Karen was a great person with a good heart. I'd met her my senior year of high school, which was her first year with child services. She was a young, pretty, optimistic social worker, and I quickly became her pet project. By the end of that year, we'd become more like sisters than anything. Much like my relationship with Jo, I knew I could tell her anything and she seemed to genuinely care about me, even gifted me with the money I needed to move to LA after graduation, no small feat for a woman with her salary. But then again, Karen had come from a life of privilege, was one of those Jack and Jill black girls who took the job with the county as her way of giving back.

It was Karen who drove me to the bus station, and right before I climbed those steps and began my journey away from Reola, Alabama, I asked if she would check on my family and keep me up-to-date with what was happening with them, especially my mother who was in jail at the time. I only knew that because it was common gossip. Since my family was so fucked up, they weren't allowed to contact me. Sure, I hated her, but I still cared for some reason. Karen had quickly and eagerly agreed, glad we'd remain in contact with one another. That was twelve years ago, and as dear as Karen had always been to me, I knew it was past time to release her from that responsibility. The woman had a husband and kids now. She didn't need to be tangled up in my family anymore.

"Waiting for an important call? Another part?"

I almost jumped right out of my shoes at the sound of his voice. Looking up, I saw that Nolan was wearing a smile on his handsome face that I didn't have the heart to return.

I shook my head and slipped the phone back into my pocket. "Uh, no. Let me get back out there since I'm supposed to be hosting this thing."

My voice must've sounded off, because he asked, "Hey, you okay?"

You're an actress. Act!

Upon receiving that internal admonishment, I flashed him my best smile and nodded. "I'm great." Then I made my exit and resumed my duties as shower hostess.

*****

"Thanks for helping, guys. I really appreciate it," I said to the five big burly men before me—Big South's security team—as they carried Jo's gifts up to the baby's unfinished nursery. That baby was coming in a couple of months and I swear the poor thing was going to have to sleep on a naked mattress on the floor at the rate Jo was going with putting that room together, but she was determined to design it herself, having turned down South's offer to hire a decorator.

I was gathering up the last few boxes to take upstairs myself when I heard a familiar voice say, "I can take those for you."

Tommy.

I gave him a smile, a sincere one, because Tommy was a good guy, a kind soul who I just wasn't compatible with. To be honest, he wasn't even my type, and I knew that from the start. I was all ambition, and work would always come first for me. Tommy was chill. He loved his job, but he was ready for the one thing I couldn't give him—a family. What we'd shared was short, intense, and fun. But it wasn't love, and we both knew that. We didn't have what it took to build a marriage, let alone a family. Then again, I wasn't looking to build one of those with anyone anyway.

"Sure," I finally said, handing him the boxes. "Thank you, Tommy."

He gave me a little nod and turned to leave. He looked good and peaceful...content, and the exchange wasn't as weird as I feared it would be, since those were the first words we'd traded since our breakup. It was...pleasant, mature, and I was grateful for that. I'd burned enough bridges for one day.

A few seconds later, I was heading to the living room to tell Jo I was leaving when I ran right into Nolan, who barely acknowledged me. Oh, well. I had too much shit on my mind to fake it for him again, anyway.

Nolan

I felt stupid as hell. I'd dragged my feet, fucked around and missed my window of opportunity. I saw her talking to Tommy-the-bodyguard after Jo's baby shower, and from the smile she wore after they ended their conversation, they were good, probably messing around again. And what messed with my head more than anything was that the thought of her being back with Tommy upset the shit out of me, had me acting all bitchish, halfway speaking to her when we crossed paths, ignoring her, and now, two weeks after the shower, I was actually avoiding her, because the sight of her legs in high heels and her ass in anything was making me lose my damn mind, and I didn't want her to see it on my face. When the hell did I develop this overwhelming desire for this woman whom I barely knew? I could count on one hand how many weeks I'd gone without sex over the years. I had never been hard up, but I'd be damned if my ass wasn't drooling over this woman like she possessed the one and only pussy in the world, and I hadn't even had a sample of it! Shit, I was losing it for real, and I had no damn idea why. Yeah, she was fine and smart and pretty and...damn. She was everything. That was the issue. Bridgette Turner was everything I'd ever wanted, but she wasn't mine, and that was the problem. That's why I was standing in a corner watching her and Honey kill the scene they were filming in my club—well, it was actually Everett's and Leland's club, but I ran it, so it was basically mine. Anyway, that was why I was standing there like a lost and hungry-ass rottweiler staring at a meaty-ass bone.

Shit, shit, shit!

I was in such a trance, I didn't even hear Laz yell cut. It still didn't register that they'd finished the scene as my eyes followed Bridgette from her mark to the craft services table. Hell, when Laz landed a heavy hand on my shoulder, I jumped and damn near shrieked.

"She fine, ain't she? That's some grade-A ass right there, bruh," he said, in a low tone.

I frowned and glanced up at him. Laz was big and tall, but not the same big and tall as my brothers. He was carrying around a spare tire and a double chin, the definition of out of shape. Talented as hell and a cinematic visionary, but he wasn't going to win any awards in the looks department. Not that he gave a damn.

"Who?" I asked, finally tearing my attention away from Bridgette.

"Honey! Who else?"

I shifted my gaze to where she'd joined Bridgette. They were laughing about something. "Yeah, she's cute," I agreed.

"Cute? Shiiiid, man...you crazy! That's some prize-winning pussy right there!"

I frowned. "You and her? Y'all are a thing?"

"No, but we will be after tonight. I guarantee it. Which reminds me. Can you hook me up with that VIP room upstairs tonight? We gonna need the privacy, if you know what I mean." He punctuated his statement by elbowing me and then laughing that loud, snorting laugh of his. "You gonna be here, right?"

"Yeah, yeah. Just ask for me when you get here. I'll take care of you," I said, letting my eyes roam the huge club again until I spotted Bridgette and Honey sitting at one of the tables.

"You always do," Laz said, before heading in the direction of the two ladies.

I shook my head and headed to my office in the club. It was early in the afternoon, and I had tons of paperwork to do before we opened our doors later that night. This first official day of filming would have to go on without my stupid ass stalking Bridgette Turner.

5

Bridgette

Jessie Mae Parker, age 68, died unexpectedly in her home in Reola, Alabama, on January 8. She was the only daughter of Augustine and Linda Jones. A lifelong resident of Reola, she attended Reola public schools and married Earl Parker while still in her teens. A homemaker, Mrs. Parker worked tirelessly her entire life to care for her family and to help those in her community. Left to cherish her memory are her brother, Augustine Jr., her daughter, Arlette, her son, Earl Jr., a special granddaughter whom she helped raise, Jessie Mae, and a host of other grandchildren, nieces, and nephews...

That was where I stopped reading the online lie-bituary for my grandmother, a term I use loosely. Jailer, warden, abuser, evil bitch? Yes. Grandmother? *Hell no.* That lie-bituary was a sweeping work of fiction chocked full of bullshit. So she was a homemaker? Riiiight. And she helped raise me? Okay. Helped the community? If you call smoking and selling crack and pimping hoes helping, then yeah.

I closed my laptop and turned my attention to the episode of *Wives with Knives* that was playing on my TV. I kept it on the ID Channel for the most part, because I'd always been a little twisted, I suppose. But who the hell could blame me with the damn hood novel existence I'd once lived. The shit I went through growing up would make those book characters' lives seem like fairy tales.

Unable to focus on my usual brand of entertainment, I leaned against my headboard, closing my eyes and trying to breathe through what I was feeling about my gr—*that woman's* passing. It wasn't sorrow or sadness, but anger. The woman was dead, and I still hated her, and that bothered me. It bothered me that even after death, she could affect my mood like this. Years had passed since I last saw her old crackhead ass, and I still despised her.

I opened my eyes, and my mind shifted to my mother, my *weak* mother who never, not once, tried to protect me from *her* mother. She just…let it happen, all of it.

And I hated her to this day for it.

She hadn't called me anymore, so there was that, but I was still off-balance and disturbed about this intrusion into my world, a world I built to block that part of my life out. I'd worked so damn hard to delete that part of my life, to forget being scared and actually seeing that youth home as a sort of paradise. Hell, anything was better than that den of crackheads I was living in. Crackheads, prostitutes, johns, perverts, hunger, nightmares…

I hopped from the bed to my feet, paced around the room while shaking my head, and when I found myself biting my expensively-manicured nails—a disgusting Jessie Mae habit I'd broken long ago—I sat back down on the bed and let a little whimper escape my throat, but I didn't cry.

I didn't cry.

Nolan

"*The Gallery.* How may I help you?"

I held the phone for more than a few seconds, so long that the familiar voice repeated her greeting.

Finally snapping out of a haze of hesitation, I said, "Heather, it's McClain."

"McClain! It's been awhile. Are you joining us this evening? Your usual time? Want me to set up your favorite room? We have some new girls I know you'll be delighted to meet. All models."

I paused again. This didn't feel right, not anymore, but shit, I was horny. So I finally said, "Yes."

"Great! Everything will be ready for you."

"Thanks."

I stared at my cell for a moment before placing it on my desk and scrubbing my hand down my face. Bridgette, or maybe my irrational desire for her, was messing with my head, had me thinking I should end my membership at *The Gallery*. And that was just crazy. That place had been a vital part of my life for years.

Shaking those thoughts off, I focused my attention on the split-screen monitor on my desk. The club was packed, including VIP, except for the room I was holding for Laz. If his ass didn't hurry up and make an appearance, he would be ass out. It was already close to midnight, and I was trying to have some fun myself. I'd give him another thirty minutes, and then I was out of there and on my way to a damn good night. I was going to make sure of that.

Fifteen minutes later, I got the call that he had arrived, left my office, and headed to VIP to escort him and Honey into their room because Laz liked that shit, thought it made him look important for the club's manager to do it rather than another club employee. He'd always been a good patron, and he was a friend, so it wasn't a big deal for me to appease him. Plus, his arrival meant my departure, so walking him to VIP wasn't an inconvenience since I'd be leaving right after that anyway.

I stopped at a few tables to speak to some regulars and went to the bar to let them know what to send up to Laz, so a few minutes had passed by the time I made it upstairs to find Laz…with Bridgette by his side.

6

Nolan

"Bridgette! Hey, Bridgette! Can you walk? Bridgette!" I shook her where she sat slumped in the passenger seat of my car, my damn heart throttling my rib cage with each beat.

Her head rolled toward me as she fought to focus her eyes on me. "Wert arf key?" she mumbled, then reached up and sloppily swiped at her mouth and tugged on her bottom lip before her head lolled to the side again.

I was so panicked, I could only think of doing one thing. So I fumbled around the center console until I felt my phone, lifted it to my face, and as the screen lit up illuminating my car's interior, I muttered, "I'ma call the police."

Her head snapped back toward me, and she frowned as she attempted to rub her forehead. "No!" she shouted clearly. "No, d-d-on't faw kip!"

"Huh? What?"

"D-d-don't calllll," she groaned.

"But-but I've got to. They need to—"

Her shaky hand clamped onto my arm. "No," she whimpered. "P-p-please. No."

I dropped the phone to my lap and closed my eyes. What the fuck was I supposed to do? This shit was all the way fucked up. She was out of it, and I didn't know why I bothered asking if she could walk when she'd barely made it out of the club and into my car on her own two feet. I was parked in my driveway, because I didn't know her address and this was the only place I could think to go, but maybe I should've taken her to Everett's place since she and Jo were close. But shit, Jo was pregnant, and from what Everett had told me, she was emotional as hell right now. It probably wouldn't be a good idea to bust in on them.

"Okay…okay, then I'm just gonna take you to the hospital, all right? They-they can help you."

Her head rolled back and forth. "No, pees-please. Just sweep. I want to sweep."

"Sweep?"

"Night-night," she slurred. "*Sweep.*"

"Sleep? You wanna sleep? Is that safe? Should you be sleeping right now?"

Nothing from her, because evidently, she'd already fallen asleep.

I slapped the steering wheel, and shouted, "Fuck!"

Bridgette didn't move a muscle.

Take her to the hospital, repeated in my head, but I couldn't erase the desperate look I saw in her eyes when she begged me not to. So, I pulled my car into my garage, and a few minutes later, carried her inside my house. After I'd laid her in my bed, I sat next to it and watched her sleep.

7

Nolan

Two hours earlier...

For a second, I just stood there and wondered what the fuck was going on. What the hell was Bridgette doing with Laz? Where was Honey? Then I told myself that this was probably a cast get-together I wasn't aware of, something to build camaraderie. Yeah, that had to be it. Otherwise, this shit didn't make sense.

"You gonna let us in?" Laz asked, eyebrows raised as he slipped an arm around Bridgette's waist.

My eyes shot from his arm to Bridgette's face. She looked...apathetic, almost as if she wasn't really present in that moment. The fuck was going on?

"Nole!" Laz said through a chuckle. "You a'ight, man?"

I blinked a couple of times and nodded. "Yeah, yeah." As I opened the door and led them in, I asked, "Honey on her way?"

He shot me an incredulous look as he allowed Bridgette to enter the room before him. "Nah, it's just me and Ms. Turner here."

Bridgette took a seat on the couch and fixed her eyes on the coffee table.

"Bridgette, you good?" I asked.

She lifted her head, basically looked through me, and nodded. Something was wrong with her, but I couldn't put my finger on it. She wasn't high. I knew what that looked like. She was just...blank, like there was nothing in there, like she was on empty.

Laz cleared his throat, and I tore my eyes away from Bridgette, focusing on him. "Oh," I said. "Uh, someone's gonna bring your regular order up from the bar."

He slapped his hand on my shoulder and smiled down at me. "Good, good."

My eyes found their way back to Bridgette. "You need anything, Bridgette? From the bar, I mean?"

She shook her head without looking up at me.

And then I just stood there, because the last thing I wanted to do was leave her alone with this nigga.

"I think we're good, man," Laz said, but I barely heard him.

My eyes were still on Bridgette as I nodded. "Yeah."

A minute or so later, Laz said, "Uh, don't they need you in your office or something?"

Shit, I needed to leave. It didn't make sense for me to still be there, but my damn feet wouldn't move. Another minute had passed before I managed to put one foot in front of the other and make my way out of the room, closing the door behind me. Then I just stood there and stared at the door until I realized the people in the roped-off VIP areas were staring at me. So I left, returning to my office instead of leaving the club, because I couldn't leave, not knowing Bridgette was up there with Lazarus. How the hell did that happen? Had he been sniffing in behind her the whole time he was acting like he wanted Honey?

I stayed in my office for an hour, watching the monitors for the VIP area and wishing there were cameras in that room with them, but Everett had wanted that one spot to have privacy for the patrons who were willing to pay top-dollar for it. Their need for privacy had worked in my favor up until this point, fattened my pockets, and made me privy to the kinds of secrets that help when you're making moves in Hollywood. I'd turned my head and played dumb about a lot of shit that went down in that room. But this time?

The last thing that motherfucker needed with her was privacy.

And the last thing I could do was turn my head and play dumb.

Motherfuck!

I sat my stupid ass up there staring at the monitors for another few minutes before I decided to just bust in there on them, because I had to do *something*. I rushed through the club so fast everything around me was a blur, and when I made it to the room, the door opened before I could touch the knob.

Lazarus didn't see me at first, because he was too busy trying to lead a very wobbly Bridgette out of the room.

"What's wrong with her?" I asked. Well actually, it was more of a bark.

Laz looked startled as his eyes shifted from her to me. "She drunk. Whatchu think wrong with her?"

"Did you give her something?" I'd heard the rumors. Shit, everyone had. It was widely known that Laz was supposed to be on that shit Bill Cosby was charged with. It had never been proven, but I'd seen him leave this room with other women who looked just as altered as Bridgette did. *I knew.* In my soul, I knew what was behind those sexual escapade stories he told. I just chose to ignore the truth.

"What?!" he shrieked. "I ain't gave this bitch nothing! She drunk, and I'm gonna take her home. The fuck is wrong with you tonight? You acting like you fucking her or something."

He tried to leave but I blocked him, and the fact that he was practically dragging Bridgette with him didn't make things any easier for him.

"Bridgette, you all right?" I asked.

Her eyes crawled up to me, and she squinted. "Nolan? Neil? Hey, y'all! You got on the same clothes? Can y'all help me? My-my-my feet won't work. Why is this place moving?" She gasped, and her eyes expanded. "I think my body is gone. I can't feel it," she whimpered. "Can y'all help me find it?"

"I'll take her home," I said.

"I got her," Laz said, while shaking his big-ass head.

"No, I got her. She's a family friend. I'll catch it if I don't help her."

"Nole, I got this—"

I moved closer to him, lowered my voice, and said, "I know you fucking drugged her just like you drugged all those other women you've brought here. There are cameras hidden in that room. If you don't leave now and let me handle this, I'm sending all the motherfucking videos to the media," I bluffed.

He stood there for a second before dropping her arm. She would've hit the floor if I hadn't caught her.

"Pussy probably ain't that good anyway," he mumbled, as he left.

If I hadn't been trying to keep Bridgette from falling, I would've knocked his ass out.

I stood there for a moment before leading Bridgette through VIP to the staff elevator. I damn near had to carry her out the back door to my car, but I got her in there, and my only thought during the ride to my house was that I wanted to break Lazarus' fucking neck.

8

Bridgette

Now...

I didn't have to open my eyes to know I wasn't in my own bed or my own home. This place didn't feel like home, and the sheets didn't smell like my favorite lavender detergent. They still smelled good, clean, but different. Finally peeling my eyes open, the first thing I saw were wooden beams overhead dividing a stark white ceiling. A turn of my head gave me a view of palm trees and ocean through a huge picture window, and I knew where I was. The previous night was foggy, but I remembered being with Lazarus Holmes, having agreed to meet him at *Second Avenue* when he called, because I needed to do something to take my mind off of my past's intrusion into my present. I didn't like him, definitely wasn't attracted to him, but I was willing to let him entertain me. I was going to have a few drinks, maybe dance a little, and then leave the club—alone, because I wasn't dumb enough to jeopardize my career by sleeping with the director of a film I was working on. I wasn't trying to be known as a Hollywood THOT.

But evidently, I *was* one, if unintentionally, because I was lying in his huge bed in his beautiful home.

Shit.

How much did I drink? I was always careful not to get drunk when I went on dates, but I guess my grandmother's passing and my reaction to it really messed my head up.

I moved my hand down my body under the soft covers—I mean, those sheets must've had a damn eight thousand thread count—and found that I still had on my clothes. *Did the motherfucker re-dress me or something after we did it? And why can't I remember us doing it? Damn, was it that bad?*

It might've been bad, but it must've been rough as hell, too, because I was sore all over, like I had the flu or something. I closed my eyes and moaned.

"You hurting?"

My eyes popped open, and I sat up a little in search of the voice's owner. I had to blink a few times to be sure I was seeing what I thought I was seeing. Nolan McClain was standing in the doorway of the enormous bedroom, bare-chested and holding a white shirt, looking so damn fine with those pecs and abs and shit that I almost forgot what was going on. I mean, shit. Nolan was just as fine as South!

"Bridgette, *are you hurting?*" he repeated.

"Yes."

I rested my hand on my gurgling stomach and moaned again.

"You need to throw up again?" he asked, rushing out the room before I could answer and quickly returning with a small, brass-looking wastebasket.

"Throw up? Nolan, what are you doing here?"

He looked just as confused as I felt. "What?"

"What are you doing here? Wait, did we have a threesome?! Did y'all run a train on me?! Oh my God!" I screeched and then fell back on the bed, closed my eyes, and gripped my forehead because the volume of my own voice made my damn head throb.

"No!" he said, sounding more than a little alarmed.

"Then what are you doing here with your damn shirt off?" I asked, eyes still closed.

"I'm here because this is my house and I'm changing my shirt. Haven't had time to take a shower, but I thought at least I should put on clean clothes."

I opened my eyes and fixed them on him again. "Your house?

Where's Lazarus?"

He stared at me. "I don't know."

"He already left?"

"Bridgette, do you remember anything that happened last night?"

Damn, was he looking for a compliment on his performance or something? "Uh...yeah."

"But you don't know how you ended up here or what happened after you got here?"

"Um..."

"You don't remember Laz drugging you?"

"What?! I..." Swinging my legs over the side of the bed—an act that hurt like hell because my legs felt like they each weighed a ton—I stared out the window and tried to recall what had happened. The more I tried, the hazier most of the night became, but I did remember drinking one drink and feeling weird afterwards. Lazarus had poured our drinks, and I was in such a depressed funk, I didn't watch him do it. I remembered it felt like my body was disintegrating after I finished my drink. I remembered him offering to drive me home, and I remembered Nolan virtually carrying me out of the club. It all came in flashes, little bits of recollections. I shared what I'd recalled with Nolan, and asked, "You brought me here?"

He nodded.

"So, I didn't have sex with Lazarus?"

He shook his head. "Not unless you did at the club. I mean...did y'all have sex at the club?"

"No...I don't think so." I inspected the white, carpeted floor and thought for another minute or two. "No, we didn't." Letting my eyes rise to meet his, I asked, "Did we...did *we* have sex?"

"What? No! I mean, not that it would've been a bad thing, but you couldn't have consented, so no. I just...I brought you here and put you to bed. Not *to* bed, but *in* my bed, and I sat here and watched you sleep, helped you when you got sick. That's it."

"Then...then thank you for that."

"You're welcome."

"Why?"

"Why what?"

"Why'd you bring me here and take care of me? Why didn't you let me leave with Lazarus?"

"Because I knew he'd drugged you and I knew *why* he drugged you."

I didn't know how to respond to that. This whole situation was upsetting as hell.

"You thirsty? Hungry?"

I nodded. "My mouth is dry. Water would be good."

He left, and when he returned, handed me a glass. "It's ginger ale. I thought that'd be better than water with your stomach like it is."

I nodded again, took a sip, let my eyes peruse the room, and said, "You sure it's okay for me to be here?"

"Why wouldn't it be? It's *my* house."

"You live alone?"

"Yeah…"

"Oh, never mind then."

"Never mind what?"

"I thought maybe your girlfriend lived here."

"No. I mean, I don't have one. You need me to call anyone? Tommy, maybe?"

"Tommy? No. Why would I need you to call him?"

"Aren't y'all…together?"

"No."

"Oh."

Silence.

"Did you say you were hungry?" he queried.

I shrugged. "If I threw up earlier, I guess I probably need to put something in my stomach."

"Okay, don't have much food here, but I'll go get you something."

"You don't have to. I can leave—" I attempted to stand and would've fallen straight to the floor had Nolan not caught me. My damn legs were like rubber. What the hell did Lazarus Holmes give me? Rat poison? And shit, Nolan smelled *so good*. I felt like crying from the confusion swirling around in my brain.

"Stay here. I'll run out and get something. Okay?" Nolan said, concern in his eyes as he peered at me.

"Okay. Thank you."

"No problem."

Nolan

The plan was to grab us something from McDonalds, something quick so I could get back to her in case she needed me, but after I started driving, I found myself passing McDonalds. Shit, I passed a bunch of restaurants, and when I finally stopped my car and looked out the windshield, I halfway couldn't remember driving there. It was like I was on autopilot or something. Like I was the dude from that movie, *Upgrade*. When I climbed out of my car and walked up to the door, it was almost as if I was outside of my body watching myself do it. I knocked, waited, and when the door swung open, I just stood there for a minute, because shit, I didn't know why I was there.

"You came to apologize for that shit you pulled last night? Long as we been boys, you coulda told me you was feeling ole girl and I wouldn't have messed with her, but instead, your ass decided to fuck my night up right when I had that pussy in the palm of my hands. I hope it was good. Tell me this: can she suck dick? She got some nice lips, so I figure she can. That's what I was on—getting my shit wet. That's why I called her after Honey said she was too busy to kick it with me..."

I frowned as this gorilla-looking motherfucker wearing nothing but a pair of boxers went on and on, saying stupid shit about Bridgette.

"...yeah, you fucked up, so you know what that means, right?

That means I get to fuck her on principle and you need to be the one to set it up."

That's when I hit his ass dead in the mouth so he would shut the hell up.

He stumbled, grabbed his mouth, said, "Nigga, are you out your mind?" and swung at me, but I ducked and came up swinging at his ass.

Yeah, he was bigger and taller than me, but he was out of shape and I was pissed the hell off, so I thrashed him over and over again, knocked him to his expensive marble floor, and started stomping his ass. Then I dropped to the floor and started punching him again. He kept yelling for help, and I knew his brother hung with him a lot, so I expected him to come pull me off this asshole and I was ready to mess him up, too, if I needed to. But the only person to show up was a little Latina woman in a t-shirt and panties who came from the direction of Laz's kitchen.

Her shriek made me stop, and my eyes focused on his bloody face. "Don't you ever fucking contact her again," I said through my teeth. "If I find out you even fucking looked at her, smiled at her, hell, if you accidentally run into her at the grocery store, I'ma have your ass killed and you know I got the connections to do it!" I looked up at the woman. "You need to raise your damn standards."

Then I turned to leave, stopped in my tracks, and squatted beside Lazarus again. "And if I hear any shit about you doing this to any other women? I'ma release that footage and make sure your ass gets locked up." I stood, rubbed my knuckles, and spit on his ass, and as I left, added, "Oh, and you're fired."

*****

"Are you going to fire me now?" Bridgette asked, breaking our mutual, eating-induced silence. Breakfast wasn't much, sausage biscuits and hash browns, but it took care of the hunger pangs.

I looked up from my food and frowned. "What? No, why would I do that?"

"Because of the thing with Lazarus. I mean, *he's* the big name. I'm just a little unknown actress. A bomb-ass actress, granted, but I don't have any clout in this town. My name won't sell any tickets. It'd make sense for you to fire me and keep him." She didn't sound upset. It was like she was used to taking lumps and moving on, like she was made of Teflon or Kevlar or something.

"That doesn't make sense to me, and that's why I fired *him*."

"You did?!"

"Yes. What happened was his fault. I'm not going to penalize you for something *he* did."

We both fell silent until I said, "I don't know if you remember, but last night, you didn't want me to call the police. Do you want to call them now?"

"No."

"Why?"

"Is that your business?" she asked, with raised eyebrows.

I reclined my neck. "Shit, my bad."

More silence and then a loud, elongated sigh from Bridgette. "Look, I'm sorry. I appreciate you rescuing me but...I just don't want this shit to overshadow my talent and my career. Reporting him won't do anything but put me in the news, lump me into this whole #metoo movement stuff. My career will die in the midst of it all, and I've barely got my foot in this Hollywood door. My career is *everything* to me. Can you please just respect my decision?"

"Yeah, I can."

"Thank you."

"Do you—I think you should at least go to the hospital, get checked out."

"They're mandated reporters. So, no to that, too."

This time, I sighed.

"So...what happened to your hand?" she asked, after she took a sip of ginger ale. She sounded like we'd just had a discussion about the weather.

I looked down at my torn knuckles and shrugged. "Nothing."

"Who'd you hit?"

"No one," I said, then took a bite of my sausage biscuit.

"Lazarus?"

"*No one.*"

"Someone posted a pic of him in the ER on IG, said he got jumped this morning."

"Did he say I jumped him?" I asked, although I knew he didn't. He knew I wasn't playing with his ass.

"No."

"Then why do you think I did?"

"Because I remembered something else from last night."

Taking a gulp of my juice, I nodded, and said, "That's good. What was it?"

"The look in your eyes when you first saw me with Lazarus. You looked shocked...and angry."

"I was," just fell out of my damn mouth.

"And the way you've taken care of me shows me you really care."

"I do." Shit, what was I saying?

"And it took you way too long to buy two McDonald's breakfast combos. So, you jumped him, didn't you?"

I sighed again. "Okay, yeah...I did."

"Why?"

Because it was you this time. "Because what he did to you was fucked up."

"And because you care about me?"

I leaned forward in the chair I had pulled up next to the bed, propping my elbows on my knees, and slid my eyes over the cups and food wrappers covering the night table. Then I let them climb up Bridgette's body from her pretty pink toenails to her hair that was a mess all over her head. "Yes, I do," I admitted.

"But you don't really know me."

"I know enough. I'd like to know more."

"But you don't like black women."

"I—"

My doorbell cut me off, so I blew out a breath, hopped up from my seat, and said, "Hold that thought. I'll be right back."

"Okay."

As I approached the front door, I could see a tall figure through the sidelight—Everett.

Shit.

As soon as I opened the door, he yelled, "We just started filming and you fired the damn director, Nole?!"

"That's fucked up," said a voice coming from behind him.

"You had to bring Neil?" I asked.

"He's my assistant again while Court is on maternity leave, and I'ma need some assistance to clean up this fuckery you got me in!"

"It's not fuckery. His ass needed to be fired! And is this why you didn't reply to my text about it? You wanted to come over here and act a fool with me?"

"First of all, you should've called instead of texting me. Second, I did call you back. You ain't been answering."

Frowning, I pulled my phone out of the pocket of my jeans. After checking the screen, I said, "Shit, I forgot I turned the ringer off after I got back home."

"Yeah, you did that shit on purpose. Look, Nole, I done put too much money into this movie for you to be doing shit off the cuff like this!"

"Hell, I put my money in it, too!" I countered.

"Then what the fuck are you doing?!"

"Yeah, what the fuck are you doing, Nole?"

"Shut up, Neil!" me and Everett shouted at the same time.

"Man, fuck y'all," Neil mumbled.

"Ev, you know me. You know I don't play about business or money, so you know I had to have a good reason to fire the motherfucker!"

"Okay, why'd you fire him?"

I lowered my voice. "He—"

"South?"

I spun around to find Bridgette hugging the foyer wall looking exhausted.

"What are you doing out of bed?" I asked, rushing to her. "You could've fallen."

"But I didn't," she rebutted.

"Aw, shit! You finally made that move, Nole?! It's about time! And thanks for giving him a chance; he been wanting your ass forever, Bridgette!" Everett shouted, then stepped closer to me, offering me some dap.

"Uh, Ev—" I started.

"I got sick last night, and Nolan's been taking care of me," Bridgette explained.

"No, Lazarus drugged her, and I caught him before he could get her out of *Second Ave*. That's why I fired his ass."

"That wasn't for you to tell!" Bridgette yelled.

"Wait, that shit about him is true?!" Neil shrieked.

"In that case, did you kick his ass, too?" Everett asked.

"Yeah," I said, responding to both Neil and Everett.

"I can't believe you told him that!" Bridgette screamed. "Hell, why don't you hit up *Tea Steepers* while you're at it?! He's gonna tell Jo, and she doesn't need to be worrying about me right now!"

"Damn, Bridgette! Do I look like a snitch?" Everett yelled.

"No! Shit! I just didn't want anyone to know!" Bridgette said, then her face folded and my fucking heart fell to pieces in my chest.

"I'm sorry, Bridgette. Ev won't tell anyone. You know he won't," I said.

She wasn't crying. I could tell she needed to but was fighting it hard. And it took everything in me not to grab her and hold her and rub her damn hair. But it didn't feel like the right time for that since she was just almost raped.

"I ain't telling shit you don't want told. You can tell Jo when you're ready. I don't need her damn emotions any more fucked up than they already are," Everett assured her.

"What about Neil?" she asked softly.

Neil stepped forward and in a gentle voice, said, "I would never spread your business, sister. I promise you that."

"Aye, Neil, man…back that up, okay?" I said.

"Why?"

I narrowed my eyes at him.

"Oh, shit! So you actually like her? You giving up the milk now? Shit, I thought you hated black women."

I stepped closer to my twin. "I ain't never said I hate black women, nigga!"

"You ain't have to say it!"

"Neil, just shut the fuck up!"

"Make me!"

"Would you two stop this shit?!" Everett thundered. "Y'all the fightingest motherfuckers in the world. The fuck is wrong with y'all?!"

"He started it. He's always starting shit!" I yelled, knowing I sounded like a kid, but Neil knew how to get under my skin better than anyone else.

"Look, if you don't want this to get out, it won't get out. Neil ain't gonna say shit unless he wants to deal with me. A'ight, Bridgette?" Everett said.

Bridgette nodded, then her eyes rounded the foyer, landing on the little table beside the door. "Is that my purse?"

I nodded. "And your keys. I had Jesse bring your car from the club, too."

She flinched.

"You okay? Hurting?"

Shaking her head, she said, "South, can you take me home?"

I almost started panicking, but kept my cool, and said, "You don't have to go. You shouldn't be alone right now, should you?"

"I'll be fine. I just…I wanna go home."

Everett looked from her to me and back. "Yeah, I got you. Neil can drive your car for you."

I wanted to beg her to stay, but I just kept quiet, realizing that it was best to let her go. So instead, I grabbed her shoes from my bedroom and helped her to Everett's SUV where Chink was sitting behind the wheel.

"Aye, I'ma call you later so we can figure out what to do about getting another director."

I nodded, but I already had that covered. Like I said, I didn't play about business, always had a contingency plan. I wished I had the same skills and awareness when it came to what I was feeling for Bridgette.

9

Bridgette

Filming on *Floetic Lustice* was suspended for a week as McClain
Films—i.e. Nolan And South—searched for another director to
replace Lazarus Holmes' sexual predator ass. Imagine my surprise
when I received an email informing me that Nolan would be taking
over as director. I'd heard he had a filmmaking degree but was
skeptical of his ability to helm this project. Then again, Nolan was a
very smart man, a thinker. He wore those qualities for the world to
see, so it shouldn't have surprised me that he was actually good at
this job that was new to him—decisive, concise with his direction,
clear on his vision for what the film should be. Firm, but kind.

I can't lie; I was feeling Nolan McClain, really feeling him now
that I knew he was feeling me. He'd kicked Lazarus' ass and then
fired him for me. *For me!* No man had ever done anything like that
before. Not even my father, and he was the one somebody that I
knew loved me despite his crippling drug addiction. If he could've
stayed out of jail, he would've protected me from that house of
horrors the county took me from.

But back to Nolan; he even made sure I was okay with being in
the club after that debacle with Lazarus Holmes, pulling me to the
side and very discreetly asking me if I needed some time off when
we first resumed filming. I assured him I was fine. I wasn't made of
paper; otherwise, I would've disintegrated long ago. So anyway,
Nolan was truly a good guy, he liked me, and I hadn't seen him with
any Russian chicks in a while. He was nice on the eyes, a younger,

shorter version of South. He had a great house, a nice car, and he cared about me, but I was too deep in my own shit to do anything about it, to reciprocate what he was offering. The death of my grandmother—an event that should have been a celebratory one for me—had plunged me into a dark place I'd worked hard to stay away from, had undergone years of therapy to cope with, and took a daily dose of Prozac just to function in spite of. But now, all I could do was remember what I'd structured my whole life around forgetting, and that was why I couldn't fully appreciate the fact that Nolan liked me.

Now, engrossed in his new duties, he was too busy to mention the whole Lazarus thing or anything else we discussed that day in his house, and that was a relief. As I sat at an empty table in *Second Avenue* with a chicken salad sandwich and a little plate of pineapple chunks I'd swiped from the craft services table and watched him talk to Nyles Adams, the male lead in the film, I thought about the blessing of this job, how at least while I was on set, I usually didn't think about my past. I also let myself think about a possible future where my mind was clear and I had something real with Nolan. Wouldn't that be nice?

He'd ended his conversation with Nyles and was heading in my direction. My first thought was to leave, because I was just fucking embarrassed about everything, but he provided such a nice view, I stayed put. His walk, so full of confidence. Nolan knew he was handsome and smart and that self-awareness turned me on.

Damn, he was fine.

My eyes followed him as he pulled up the chair next to mine at the small, round table, placed his plate before him, and took a bite of his sandwich. When he looked up at me, he gave me a wink and then went in for another bite. In response, I smiled at him and took a bite of my own sandwich. We sat there and ate in silence until break time was over, and it was the nicest meal I'd had in a long time.

*****

"Let's go out tonight," Sage nearly screamed into the phone. This girl had always had an issue with controlling the volume of her voice, but since I was perpetually on edge because of the current shitty state of my life, the volume seemed amplified.

So I replied with, "Why are you yelling?"

"Aw, shit, what's wrong with you? You don't start messing with me about how I talk until you're in a bad mood. Who did it?"

"I'm not in a bad mood. You're about to bust my damn ear drums!"

"Whatever. So are we going out or what?"

"Sage, I've been spending all my time in a club lately, working on this film. I don't really feel like being in one when I'm off."

"Oh, shit! I forgot to ask you how that's going! You met that fine-ass Nyles Adams, yet? Girl, I don't even like poetry, but I'd pay top dollar just to sit in the audience and stare at that man! You know I got a thing for men with cornrows."

"Yeah, I did a scene with him today. It was a scene where my character threatens him over her BFF. I had to basically threaten to cut his balls off if he hurt her."

"Oh, so you're playing yourself?"

"I ain't never done nothing like that!"

"You offered to do something like that to Sid for Jo."

"That was warranted, though."

"True. Anyway, sounds good! I can't wait to hit the red carpet for the premiere. How's the makeup artist on set?"

"Good, I guess."

"They could've hired me. I'd kill to do Honey's makeup!"

"Bitch, you were the one who committed to doing the makeup for that off-off-off-off-*off* Broadway play. That was *your* bad!"

"They could've worked around that!"

"Naw, Nolan ain't the 'work around that' type. He doesn't play when it comes to schedules and timeliness and stuff like that."

"You act like that's your man or something, like you really know him."

I rolled my eyes. "So why are you trying to go out? Trouble with

Gavin?"

"Why does there have to be trouble with him for me to want to go out?"

"Because I know you."

"Well, it's not Gavin."

"What is it, then?"

"Shit, *life*."

"Is life what had you crying at Jo's shower?"

I could hear her sigh. "Yeah…"

"I feel you. I really do, but girl, I don't feel like going out to—wait a sec. Let me see who's calling me." My stomach dropped when I saw the now-familiar Alabama number on my phone's screen. My grandmother's funeral had passed weeks ago. Why the hell was this woman calling me?

"Who is it? You need to hang up with me?" Sage asked.

"Uh, nobody. Hey, you know what? I *do* want to go out tonight, but not to *Vault*."

"Okay. *The Launch Pad*?"

"Yeah, or *Second Avenue*."

"Ooooh, *Second Avenue*! And you know we can get in there free since the bouncer knows we're Jo's friends. Let me get ready. You're gonna pick me up, right?"

"Yeah, I got you."

10

Nolan

"So you're really doing it? You proposed?" I asked, probably sounding just as skeptical as I felt.

"Yeah! It's time, man. We're getting old. Shit, I want at least one son and I ain't tryna be out at the baseball park in a wheelchair, talking 'bout, 'Way to go, Junior!'" Mike replied.

"Wow."

"Wow, what?"

I shrugged as I looked up at one of my best friends, another guy I'd known since college. "I mean, weren't you the one who said marriage was nothing but a piece of paper and that it was an unbeneficial trap for men? Plus, you just started seeing this girl a few months ago. Seems like things are moving pretty fast, man."

"Damn, man...I said that shit a long time ago!"

"Last year is a long time ago?"

"That wasn't no damn last year."

"Yeah, it was."

He waved me off. "You tripping, and I've known her long enough to know I want to spend the rest of my life with her. If you held on to a woman for longer than a week, you would understand what I'm talking about."

I already do. "If you say so."

"Man—"

What I knew to be Jesse's signature knock cut Mike off. "Yeah!" I shouted through the door, even though he probably couldn't hear me over the music that was absent in my sound-proof office.

A second or two later, he opened the door and peeked his head inside. "Sorry to interrupt, but I wanted to let you know I put Jo's friends in VIP."

I frowned. "Who?"

"Your sister-in-law's friends. You know, the one who's in the movie and the short one."

Bridgette is here?

Before I knew it, I was on my feet and heading out the door, having forgotten Mike was in my office or that we were in the middle of a conversation. And when he shouted, "I guess I'll catch you later. Don't forget about the party," I just yelled back, "Yeah!"

I took the staff elevator up to VIP, because it would've taken too long to wade through the crowd and I needed to get up there ASAP, because…shit, I don't know. To make sure there were no dudes with them, like I could do shit about it if there were? Hell, she wasn't my woman, and since I kicked a man's whole ass over her like she *was* my woman, she most likely would never want me in that way.

But I still wanted the shit out of her.

I almost passed her, thinking Jesse had put them in the room, not one of the roped-off areas, but there they sat on one of the couches, drinks in hand, laughing at something. From that angle, I had a perfect view of her—long legs exposed in a short skirt, high heels on, perfection. Taking a deep breath and willing myself not to act dumb in front of her as I usually did, I approached them, and said, "Here all day and still not sick of this place?"

Bridgette

My eyes shot up to him, taking him in from head to toe. He looked nice and put-together, as usual, in black or maybe navy-blue slacks and a blue and white striped shirt with a white collar and cuffs. He was smiling down at us, and I couldn't help but to smile back.

"Hey, Nolan!" Sage chirped in that enthusiastic way that belonged strictly to her.

"Hey, Sage, Bridgette."

"Hi," I said, feeling something bubbling up inside of me that I couldn't quite name. Excitement? Or relief, like maybe I'd suggested we come here on the off-chance that I'd run into this man? But I didn't do stuff like that...did I?

"Join us!" Sage suggested, and Nolan's eyes shifted from her to me, as if silently seeking my approval. I quickly gave it to him by way of a tiny nod.

He sat on the sofa across from ours, leaned forward, and rested his elbows on his knees, his eyes never leaving me. "So, are you ladies enjoying your night here so far?"

"Oh, yeah! We always have a good time here! Y'all always take good care of us!" Sage said.

With my eyes glued to Nolan, I agreed, "Yeah, you really do." I hoped he got the full meaning of my words.

"Good to know," Nolan said, with a smile.

"Oh, this is my song!" Sage yelled, springing to her feet. "I'ma go hit the floor. You coming?"

Without looking up at her, I shook my head. "No, you go ahead."

After she left, Nolan and I kind of just sat there staring at each other until he said, "You look nice."

"Thank you. So do you. But then again, you always do."

"Really?" he said, with a huge grin brightening his face. "Thank you. I haven't ever seen you slacking, either."

"Well, thanks again."

More silence, then Nolan said, "Bridgette, do you mind dancing with me?"

"Do I mind? Not at all."

Nolan stood and reached for my hand, licking his lips when I got to my feet in front of him. "Yeah, you definitely look nice."

Why did that make me feel all giddy inside?

With my hand in his, I followed him through VIP, down the stairs, and to the dancefloor in time to catch the end of Sage's song—The Internet's *Dontcha*. I was bummed we'd missed the song, because I liked the beat and was prepared to gently back it up on Nolan. Then *Boo'd Up* began to play and the whole damn crowd started singing along with it.

Nolan grinned at me. "Man, this is my song right here!"

"Sounds like it's everybody's song!" I replied.

We both laughed and he released my hand, opening his arms to me. "Shall we?"

Stepping into his embrace, I swear I heard him breathe a satisfying sigh as I wrapped my arms around the solid body that was hidden under his clothes and he rested his hands on my back, holding me close. We swayed to the song, chest to chest. Well, I was actually a little taller than him in my heels, but it still felt nice to be in his strong arms, to feel him holding me, to be enveloped by the warmth of his body.

"You feel nice, too," he whispered in my ear, the vibrations of his baritone voice traveling all the way to my core and making me feel nervous as hell.

"S-so do you." Yeah, being in his arms was messing with me, had me stuttering and shit.

We danced through the entire song, and by the time it got to that little spoken part Ella Mai does at the end, my yoni had transformed into a flowing river of estrogen and I knew without a doubt that if Nolan McClain asked for some, I would've bent over right there on that dancefloor and thrown it back for him.

As The Carters' *Ape Shit* began to fill the club—a horrible segue on the part of the DJ—Nolan released me, looked me in the eye, and was only able to say, "Bridgette," when someone, a member of the club's staff, tapped him on the shoulder and whispered something in his ear.

Giving me a regretful look, he said, "I've got to take care of this. I'll catch you later?"

I nodded and watched him leave the dancefloor, standing there through half the song before hitting the bar and rejoining Sage in VIP. I didn't see Nolan again that night.

11

Bridgette

We were filming in Nolan's home, which through un-drugged eyes, proved to be a literal showcase of luxury, a beautiful house in a masculine-without-being-dark-and-heavy way. Wood floors, huge windows, filled with shades of tan and blue. I loved it!

The scene was of a house party located at a fictional Hollywood bigwig's home where Jazz and Brother—Nyles Adams' character— would bump into each other. Jazz was to serve as the party's DJ, and as her BFF, I was there for moral support. I only had a couple of lines but had delivered them with my signature attitude and finesse and was now observing Honey and Nyles in action. When I first heard Honey was playing the lead, I rolled my eyes, figuring this was yet another colorist casting, but she actually had acting chops and was a super sweet person. I watched them banter back and forth, and then the smooth as silk Brother went in for a kiss and my heart melted like I didn't know they were acting. Cutting my eyes to the left, I noticed Trevia Adams, Nyles' wife and our costume designer, observing the scene, too, with a crazy look in her eyes. I'd heard she didn't play about her man and hoped Honey was safe. But she'd been cool thus far, and her clothing design skills were ridiculous! I was tempted to steal the outfits she'd been dressing me in.

Nolan yelled, "Cut!" and the crew broke out in applause, including me, because that scene was excellent! I truly believed that with the right promo and distribution, we had a hit on our hands.

I watched Nolan as he had a hushed discussion with Nyles and

Honey, and my mind reverted to that dance we'd shared just a couple of nights earlier, how good he'd felt and smelled, and what it did to my mind and body. I'd been thinking about him ever since and about the possibility of being with him, and at that moment, as I watched him do his director thing, I could feel myself beginning to overheat, so I stepped out of the room full of extras and film crew and lights and retreated to his kitchen where craft services had set up. I was staring at a tray of cookies when I heard a voice say, "Quite a spread today, huh?"

Nolan.

Spinning around, I was met with a smile I couldn't return, and I guess I was looking a little too serious for him, because he said, "You all right?"

My response was, "No."

"What's wrong?" When I didn't reply, his eyes roamed the room and then landed on me with a spark of recognition in them. "I'm sorry about the other night. A guy ran up a huge tab at the bar and his card was declined and he was acting a fool. I had to call the police and—"

"You say you like me, care about me, then why haven't you asked me out?"

Raising his neat, thick eyebrows, he said, "What? I-uh-I was giving you time after the whole Lazarus thing. Plus, you went off on me for telling Ev."

"I'm over the whole you telling my business thing. I mean, South is basically my brother, so I guess I might have kind of overreacted."

"Okay, but I also thought maybe I freaked you out by kicking Laz's ass."

"I love that you did that for me, and I am extremely grateful to you for firing him."

"You're welcome. Um, Bridgette, I wasn't sure if you were even attracted to me."

"I'm *very* attracted to you, Nolan."

"You are?"

"Yes. Don't act like you don't know you're fine."

"Not half as fine as you."

"So, you think I'm fine, you care about me, and you're standing right in front of me. Negro, ask me out!"

"Shit, okay! Go out with me. Tonight. *Please*."

"What time should I be ready for you to pick me up?"

"Eight."

"Okay, I'll text you my address."

"Thank you."

"You're welcome."

Then we both stood there and almost simultaneously burst into laughter. For the rest of that day of filming, I wore a smile, excited about this night out with him.

He was smiling, too.

*****

"I'm so exthited! You and Nolan! It's like a thream come prue for me!" I knew Jo was like eight thousand months pregnant and couldn't help her huge appetite, but the constant chewing and smacking in my ear, along with her full-mouth speech impediment, were testing all of my damn patience.

Nevertheless, to keep from sending her into one of her frequent crying fits, I said, "A dream come true? How?"

"Well, we're besthies, right? Sisthers in all the ways that mather. Wouldn't it be cool if we were married to bwothers?!" *Chew, chew. Smack, smack.*

"Married? It's only a date, a date I had to coerce him into making. I don't think marriage is on the agenda for us. I just hope this night is a nice one."

Slurrrrrp! Chew. Smack. "I can thream if I want to!"

"Okay, nut case. Look, I gotta finish getting ready, so I'll call you later."

I actually heard her swallow before she said, "Yeah, I need all the details!"

About thirty minutes later, he picked me up in his white Jag, and once I was inside it, it held a vague familiarity for me. But it wasn't the car I usually saw him drive—a black Camaro. Then I realized this was the car he'd taken me home in the night of Laz's attempted date rape. I had to quickly erase those thoughts from my mind so they wouldn't ruin what I hoped would be a good night.

We were both quiet as he drove us from my little Atwater Village apartment towards Malibu with Kanye West's *College Dropout* album filling the car. I wondered if he was taking me to his place, then decided against that. He probably thought that would freak me out, but it wouldn't. I felt safe with Nolan, and feeling safe was a big thing for me. It was a feeling that was foreign to me for most of my childhood, from my time with my family to the two or three foster homes I stayed in until I was placed in the group home. Who'd think a group home would prove to be my saving grace and allow me to meet my best, oldest, and dearest friend on the planet? Blessings truly come in strange packages sometimes. The Teema Jane Smith Community Youth Home was that blessing for me, along with Karen, whom I'd shut out of my life.

I sighed as I observed the gorgeous neighborhood outside the passenger window. Yeah, I shouldn't have treated her like that. I needed to fix that.

"You okay over there? I know it's taking me a minute to get to our destination, but I promise it'll be worth it."

I turned and gave him a small smile. "I'm fine. It's not like it's ever quick or easy to get from A to B in LA. I was just…thinking."

"About what? If you don't mind me asking…"

"What made you want to change teams?" It wasn't what was on my mind, but it was a question I wanted the answer to.

"Change teams?" he asked, his eyes darting from the road to me and back.

"From the time I first met you that Thanksgiving in Texas when South and Jo first got together, I've only seen you with white women. I'm just saying, I'm not white."

"I know that."

"So...why?"

"Why do I like you?"

"Yeah."

"What's not to like, Bridgette?"

I kind of blushed, or at least I blushed as much as was possible for me. "So you like black women?"

This time, he sighed. "I wish I knew why everyone assumes I don't."

I turned to fully face him, eyes wide as I said, "Uh, because the only women we've seen you with have been very white!"

"Did it occur to you that there was a reason for that?"

"Yeah...that you didn't like black women."

"How about a reason other than that? Because I love the shit out of black women."

"A black woman hurt you or something?" I threw up my hands. "Help me out here!"

"Is it really that important to you? Does it really matter? You know I like *you*, that I care for *you*, that I'll kick ass for *you*. I've never done that for any white woman."

"So you're not going to tell me?" I asked. This cryptic shit was beginning to work my last nerve.

He fell silent and I just shook my head, said, "You know what? Never mind. You're right. It doesn't matter. I was just curious," and let the subject drop.

We had arrived at our destination—a Hawaiian-themed restaurant I'd heard good things about that was located right on the water— taken our seats, placed our orders, and had been served our drinks (pineapple vodka for me; Hahn brandy for him), when he said, "I was fourteen when Everett's career took off, in the middle of puberty, and I already lacked individuality because I was a twin. Shit, half our relatives referred to us as "twin" when we were growing up, like we didn't have names, because our mom and dad— when he was alive—were the only ones who could tell us apart. Then all of a sudden, I had this famous brother and people wanted to be my friend only because of that. Girls acted like they liked me just for what they hoped was the chance to get close to Ev. In a way, it was cool being popular, and people at our school actually started making an effort to tell which one of us was which, because we were Big South's little brothers. We got invited to all the parties, Ev made sure we had the best clothes and shoes, and shit, we were living the high school dream. Had girls left and right. We were having too much fun to see how fucked up it was that all of this was only a result of Ev's fame.

"Anyway, time went on, and Neil and me started developing as individuals more and more, making it easy for us to be seen as two people instead of a matched set. We started growing apart, had our own friends and stuff. We left for college and matured a little, and I, for one, got tired of the girls who got with me in order to get to Ev. The shit just got more and more ridiculous as time went on. I only dated black girls back then, and every single one of them would get with me, be cool for a while, and then start asking when they'd get to meet Ev. The shit was actually demeaning, like my dick was a backstage pass to my brother. I just..." He paused and shook his head. "Hell, I just wanted someone to like me for me. That's all I wanted, but I couldn't find it in any of the women I dated."

"So you switched to white women?"

He nodded. "American ones at first, but then Leland got drafted into the NBA and shit really got crazy. The damn white girls were after him *and* Ev. Don't get me wrong; I love my brothers and none of this was their fault. It was just a fucked-up hand of cards I was dealt being the average, everyday brother of two famous men. Women couldn't see me for me, and I got tired of that shit, but at the same time, I didn't...I hate being alone."

"So you switched to foreign women..." I said, coming to understand his plight. I could only imagine just how difficult it must've been to exist in the shadow of two extraordinary brothers. No wonder Neil was so fucked up.

"Yeah. They have no idea who Ev or Leland are, so it's—it *was* a win for me. Hell, *I* was famous as far as they were concerned."

"So what makes you think I'm any different from the black women you dated in the past?"

He adjusted in his seat, adopting a relaxed posture in that charcoal gray suit that fit him like a damn pair of leather gloves. "I've seen you around Ev and Leland. You barely notice them. You don't seem starstruck at all."

I shrugged. "Because I'm not. I mean, I was the first few times I was around South, but that's my best friend's man. Of course I'm not checking for him, and as far as Leland goes? We all know I'm not his type, and I'm not one to pursue a man who doesn't want me. And shit, he's married now. I'm not side chick material."

"So you're attracted to my brothers?"

"I'm attracted to all y'all. Hell, I'd be attracted to your sister if I swung that way. You McClains are some gorgeous people. But look, I can be attracted to a person and not try to get with them."

He smiled, but before he could say another word, our dinner was served and we both dug in.

Nolan

"This is nice," Bridgette said, as we walked along the beach, not far from the restaurant. One of her hands was encased in mine while the other held her sandals. She was beautiful in her pink dress, the moonlight bouncing off her brown skin.

Damn.

"Yeah, it is," I agreed.

"Is it crazy that I've been living in LA for twelve years and have only been to the beach a handful of times?"

"No, I think we tend to take the things that are most accessible to us for granted."

"Hmm, you might be right."

"I usually am."

She shot me a grin. "Okay, sir. I hear you."

I chuckled as we walked in silence, and then broke it with, "Bridgette, can I ask you something?"

"Sure."

"What happened with you and Tommy? You two were going strong for a while there."

Shrugging, she replied, "It just wasn't meant to be. We weren't compatible, and to be honest, my dedication to my career is too much for most men to handle."

"Really? That's one of the things I like most about you. You are a phenomenal actress, so the dedication is definitely paying off."

"Thank you, and you are beasting this director thing. I mean, damn!"

We both laughed, and I said, "Thank you. I'm trying."

"So, I hear you're the man to go to, to learn about investing? Jo says you're a master at it and you definitely have the lifestyle to prove it."

I shrugged. "Yeah, I'm pretty good at investments, better at making beneficial connections."

"What do you mean by that?"

"Well, when Ev and Leland bought the club, I asked to manage it because I knew the type of people who'd be patronizing it. You know, music industry heavy-hitters, Hollywood insiders. I knew if I could connect with them, I could get my foot in any door I wanted to enter, and I was right."

"Like who? I mean, how do you work those connections?"

"Okay, you know who Stephanie Paré is, right?"

"Yeah, she's one of those spoiled brat socialites—tall, anorexically thin, white, blonde, famous for no reason, sexually fluid. Her dad runs *2:22 Records*."

"Right. So she came to the club one night a few years back. That's when she was dating that Baldwin chick, before she got with Talent the Prodigal One."

"Yeah…"

"So, she and her girlfriend came in there and I put them in the VIP room. They were up there an hour or two before I started getting reports of shouting and crashing coming from in there. I rushed up there to find the two of them high out of their minds and beating the shit out of each other, bloody and bruised the hell up. They tore the room up, had already run through thousands of dollars worth of liquor, and while my security was trying to pull them apart, Stephanie Paré pulled out a knife and threatened to 'Fuck all of us up if we didn't let her finish kicking that bitch's ass.'"

"Damn!"

"That's what I said. I could've called the police. Shit, I probably *should've* called them, but Ev knows her father, so I got his information from him, called and told him what was going on, and he had his people handle it, even covered the cost of repairing everything in the room. After that, he owed me a debt. I'm cashing it in at his lodge in a couple of weeks."

"The place in Montana where we're filming the girls' glamping trip? That's his?"

"Yep, and he's letting us film and stay there for free; otherwise, it would've been out of our budget."

"Wow, so stuff like that happens all the time? You sweep stuff under the rug and these rich folks end up owing you?"

"Yeah, and most of them are good about honoring their word."

"I bet they are if they don't want stuff like that getting out. Smart, Mr. McClain. Kind of blackmailish, but smart."

"I never said I was a saint."

"And I never said I wanted one."

Aw, shit! That's what I'm talking about! "So, did you enjoy your dinner?"

"Yes, and the company."

"Then you'd be willing to do this again?"

"Most definitely."

"Good."

A little over an hour later, we were standing in front of her door, and I couldn't take my eyes off her. "You really are beautiful; you know that?"

She gave me a wide smile and nodded. "I do now."

"Hmm, I better let you go inside and get your beauty rest. You don't wanna be late for work in the morning. I hear your director is an asshole."

"Shh, he might hear you."

I chuckled, and then leaned in and kissed her softly on the lips. "See you in the morning, Bridgette."

"Good night, Nolan."

12

Bridgette

"Your skin is so pretty! I mean, you can tell you take your skin care seriously. No bumps or anything. You know, it's rare for me to run across skin this smooth, and I have beat tons of faces. Tons!"

Dani, the film's makeup artist, was a sweetheart. She really was, but Lord knows she could run her mouth, and I was almost too busy staring at Nolan across the room to pay attention to what she was saying. Yeah, I was really feeling him after our date the night before, feeling him and wanting to get to know him even deeper, maybe even pick his brain more. He was nothing if not intriguing to me.

"...you should see her skin up close! Horrible! You can tell she's been living hard. The skin tells no lies," Dani continued.

"Who?" I asked, returning to our lopsided conversation.

"Honey," she whispered harshly. "Girl, it's like peanut brittle! Gotta be drugs."

"Really?" I hated gossiping about Honey. She'd been nothing but kind to me, but it wasn't like I was known to turn down some hot tea. "It's that bad?" I added.

"Yeah! And it's not just regular acne or from greasy foods. I've been in this business long enough to know the difference. Child, that's heroin and brown liquor skin. I'm telling you!"

"Damn," I said under my breath, as I let my gaze shift from my potential man to Honey Combs. She was so pretty and successful. Why would she need to be living so hard?

We were filming at the McClain Films building on a set decorated to look like Jazz's—the main character's—apartment living room. In this scene, Jazz and my character were supposed to be chilling at her apartment when Brother drops by. My character says something sassy and makes a quick exit, but even though I'd only be onscreen for a few minutes, I still had to undergo the "Cynthia" transformation of makeup, hair, and wardrobe, not that I minded. I'd always loved playing dress-up and make-believe. That was probably what made me a good actress—my love for it.

"Delivery for Bridgette Turner?!"

My head snatched to the right so fast, Dani damn near put my eye out with her mascara wand.

"Sorry," I said, scrambling from the chair to my feet and rushing over to the man who had just stepped onto the set holding a massive bouquet of lilac-colored roses.

As I approached him, he said, "Bridgette Turner?"

I nodded a little too enthusiastically. "Yeah, that's me."

He handed me the heavy bouquet and nodded before leaving me standing there grinning like a complete and utter fool. I turned toward Nolan, who was staring at me but soon returned my smile. After digging the card out and reading his words, I held my hand to my chest and smiled even harder.

Bridgette,

Have you ever met someone whose soul pairs so well with yours that you wonder how you've managed to survive this life without knowing them? That's how I felt last night.

You made me smile more than I have in a long time, and I can't seem to get you off my mind (not that I want to). Looking forward to more dinners, more conversations, and more smiles with you.

Nolan

When I looked in his direction again, he gave me a wink before resuming his director duties, and I floated back to Dani's chair as she bombarded me with questions about who sent the flowers to me. To which I answered, "Hell, Mr. Right, I think."

Might be time to pack up my yoni wand.
Yesssssss!

*****

"I'm so jealous! You could've come over here to get ready for this date! I miss you! Just because I'm on maternity leave from business now doesn't mean you can't come see me. And Nat's been asking about you, too," Jo whined through the speakers of my phone as I talked to her while playing Candy Crush.

"I been busy acting and shit."

"And, dating your director."

"Jo, this is only the second date."

"But you said y'all been eating lunch together every day this week."

"Because we're on set together. It's not like we're putting forth a lot of effort to have lunch together."

"Still, you're spending time together, talking, getting to know each other. Next thing you know, I'ma be your matron of honor."

"Me, too!" Sage chimed in as she worked on my face. I preferred her work to Dani's, because she had a much lighter touch. Dani applied makeup like it was for the stage instead of a film.

"You'll be the maid of honor, Sage, since you're not married," Jo corrected.

"Damn, rub it in, why don't you?" Sage muttered.

"Shit, I lost this level againnnnn!" I groaned.

"You know, I should be insulted that you're playing a damn game while talking to me," Jo said.

"I should be insulted that she's playing this game while I do her makeup, got her damn head down…" Sage complained.

"You two heifers know what? I don't have time for y'all. Jo, I will come visit you tomorrow morning, so you need to have me some breakfast ready. Now let me hang up and put this phone down before I have to hurt Sage."

"Fine, bye," Jo said.

"Bye!" I replied.

"I can't believe she wasn't eating," Sage observed.

"Girl, she probably ate before she called to keep me from talking about her," I said.

Sage laughed. "You probably right!"

An hour later, Nolan opened the passenger door of his Jag and offered me his hand, helping me to my feet outside the Beverly Hills Sable Inn. As he had when I opened my apartment door for him, he eyed me from head to toe and licked his lips before clutching my hand in his, handing the valet his keys, and leading me through the posh lobby to the ballroom where his friend's engagement party was to be held.

I was wearing a downright disrespectful little plum-colored, one-shouldered dress that fell just above my knees and had asymmetrical draping that gave the illusion of me wearing a cape. With it, I paired gold Bentley ankle-tie stilettos. My heels put me a little taller than him, and knowing they would, I had been hesitant to wear them since some men could be weird about that. But judging from the look in Nolan's eyes every time they skirted over my body, he didn't mind at all.

As he rested a hand on the small of my back, leading me to our table in the packed room, I soothed my hand over my sleek bob and let my eyes take in my surroundings from the white fabric draped from the ceiling and walls to the white tablecloths and gold centerpiece arrangements. Whoever this friend of his was, he'd spared no expense to celebrate his engagement.

We'd only been sitting at the huge, round table a couple of minutes before we were joined by other couples until all the seats were eventually filled. Everyone was cordial, but I could quickly tell none of the couples knew each other.

Nevertheless, I leaned in close to that good-smelling-ass Nolan, and asked, "You know any of these people at this table?"

"Nah, Mike's an investment banker, so I assume they're some of his clients or maybe some of his fiancée's friends and family."

"Hmm," I said, giving him a little nod.

He moved in closer, letting his mouth graze my ear as he said, "You look beautiful, by the way. Absolutely beautiful," and backed away enough to lock eyes with me.

I looked into his dark eyes and smiled. "Thank you. Um, you don't mind that the shoes make me so tall?"

Closing the space between us again, he murmured, "Shidddd, that's the best part, makes those legs of yours look a mile long."

"Well, that's good, because I have a closet full of stilettos."

"And short dresses?"

"Mm-hmm…"

"*Damn.*"

"What the hell is going on here?! I know this ain't Nolan McClain all up in a sister's face! And a fine one, too! You lost, bruh?" The voice belonged to a tall guy built like a damn linebacker. He wore a very expensive suit and a genuinely shocked expression as he towered over Nolan.

"Man, fuck you!" was Nolan's response. "I come to help you celebrate your engagement and you make it your business to fuck with me?"

"Shit, I'm serious! Did you run out of Russian girls? The hell you doing here with her?"

Nolan snaked an arm around my shoulders, pulling me close to him. "Mike Otobo, this is my date, Bridgette Turner. Bridgette, this is one of my oldest friends and a certified asshole, Mike Otobo. This is his party. I'm sure the woman he somehow convinced to marry him is around here somewhere."

This Mike guy just stood there and stared at me, open-mouthed.

"Damn, Mike. You gonna say hello?"

Mike stepped closer to me and extended his hand. "It is nice to meet the woman who drug this nigga back over to the dark side. I mean, congratulations, sister. Shit, you want a seat at the head table?"

"Nigga, if you don't take your silly ass on!" Nolan said.

Mike finally broke character and howled with laughter. "I'm just fucking with y'all, but I really am lowkey shocked. Damn, when you decided to cross the tracks, you went straight to the good neighborhood."

"Mike, man. I'ma leave if your ass don't stop."

"Naw, man, don't leave. I'm glad y'all made it. I'ma hit you up later to find out how this happened, but right now, I got more guests to greet. Oh, wait! Here's my lady..."

He introduced us to his lovely fiancée, Iyla, an actress I'd seen at a few auditions before, but she didn't seem to recognize me, not that I cared. Nolan had me feeling too giddy to be concerned about anything. Add that to the fact that I hadn't received any disturbing phone calls in a few days, and I was feeling great.

After Mike and Iyla left to continue their party-hosting obligations, Nolan said, "I'm sorry about that. Mike is a damn clown."

"He's funny. Tickled the shit out of me."

"Yeah..."

"You know, if you keep seeing me, you'll probably get more reactions like that from people given your past dating practices."

"*If* I keep seeing you? Unless you say otherwise, there's no question about that. I thought I made that clear in my note."

"I read the note, but I wasn't sure how many more dinners and smiles you wanted to share with me. I mean, what if you change your mind about me, revert back to your old ways?"

"I won't."

"You sure about that?"

"Let me show you how sure I am," he murmured, and then gently pressed his lips to mine.

When he backed away from me, all I could say was, "Okay."

Right at that moment, I was twerking internally from the vibes he was giving me, feeling all nervous, and shit, hopeful that this thing with him could become a *real* thing. And later on, when we hit the dancefloor? Wow! Nolan could move. I mean, the slow dance we'd shared at the club that night was nice, and I could tell he had rhythm, but I'd never seen him *dance* dance before despite us attending a lot of the same events and McClain family gatherings. That night, he cut loose at his friend's engagement party. He was smooth and sexy as hell, grabbing my hips and grinding on me to Galimatias' *South*. Nolan was *nasty*, and by the time we left the floor, I was about ready to propose marriage to him.

Yeah, that Nolan McClain was something else.

*****

"Coffee or tea?" Nolan drawled into the phone. It was late, and neither of us wanted to hang up despite the fact that we both had to be on set early in the morning. We hadn't seen each other outside of work for a few days and I suppose we were missing each other. This was my first time hearing any hints of his Texas upbringing in his voice. I guessed tiredness brought it out.

"Light-skinned coffee," I answered.

"Oh, you one of those baby coffee drinkers, huh?"

"Don't hate. Dressing or stuffing?"

"I'm from Texas. You know damn well I don't call it stuffing, and neither does your Alabama ass."

"Touché."

"Uh-huh…Brian McKnight or Trey Songz?"

"Nigga, really?"

"I need your answer, and if we're gonna keep seeing each other, it better be right."

I was grinning as I lay there in my bed with my eyes closed. "Brian McKnight!"

"Whew, okay. Thought I was gonna have to delete your number, fire you from the movie, avoid you on the street—"

"Whatever! Jelly or preserves?"

"I'm from the country, Bridgette."

"Me, too. So you better get this right."

"Preserves, of course. Cable or Netflix?"

"Since I gotta have the ID Channel and I love me some *Insecure*, I have to say cable."

"ID Channel? Damn, okay."

I chuckled into the phone. "Armani or Hugo Boss?"

"We talking suits?"

"Yeah."

"Hugo Boss, hands down."

"Was that suit you wore to your friend's engagement party a Hugo Boss?"

"Yeah."

"Shit, I agree, then."

He laughed. "Well, thank you."

"Pumpkin pie or sweet potato pie?"

"Okay, first of all, that's an insulting-ass question. And second, it was my turn," Nolan said.

I stifled a giggle. Yeah, he made me *giggle*. "My bad. Go ahead, pumpkin lover."

"I'll be damned if that's so. Me or Idris Elba?"

I snorted a laugh into the phone. "What?!"

"Me—five-eleven, one hundred and eighty pounds of brown muscle. Or that other dude with the accent who makes movies and shit. I mean, I make movies too. So, we're basically the same."

"I'll take the five-eleven movie maker for one hundred, Alex. I don't think Idris is all that anyway."

"You're lying."

"I am, because he's finer than a motherfucker, but so are you, Nolan. Fine as hell, and readily accessible. I definitely choose you."

"Is that right?"

"Yeah."

"Glad to know you think I'm fine, because I think you're gorgeous. I could lose myself in you, you know that?"

Daaaaamn. "You could?"

"Yeah. You're like…you're perfect."

"No, I'm really not, Nolan," I said softly.

"You are to me. Absolutely perfect."

I didn't know how to respond to that, but he rescued me by saying, "I'ma let you go now. See you in the morning, Bridgette."

"Night, Nolan."

13

Nolan

"You comfortable?" I asked, as we lay side by side on the floor.

"I'm good. Just wasn't expecting to be lying on the floor of this place, but I guess this would provide the best view," she replied, adjusting herself on her mat.

"Yeah. You ever been to one of these before?"

"A planetarium? No. Never crossed my mind to come to one. You?"

"Yeah, a while back. Neil used to really be into stars and space and stuff, so Uncle Lee took us to a planetarium in Houston one time when we were kids."

"Uncle Lee? You're bullshitting me!"

I chuckled as she turned her head and grinned at me. "Believe it or not, Uncle Lee really stepped up and helped my mom with us after my dad died. He was like Ev's backup. Now, he was cursing the whole time we were there, but he took us."

She laughed. "I know he *had* to cut up. Wouldn't be Uncle Lee if he didn't."

Before I could agree with her, the person running the program or show for that night began to speak about light pollution and how the constellations are hidden from us because of it and some other stuff. When his spiel was over, he killed the lights in the room, and a few twinkling stars were projected onto the dome-shaped ceiling.

"This is what we see in the city. Not much, is it?" the host said. "And this is what you'd see without the light pollution."

Projected onto the ceiling now were tons of twinkling lights.

Gasps and squeals filled the room, and I had to admit that it was beautiful, breathtaking. Turning my head, I could see Bridgette lying there with her mouth open, her eyes glued to the ceiling.

We saw the solar system, asteroids, and the individual stars of the constellations before the images panned out to show the entirety of each constellation—Orion, Cygnus, Scorpio, Leo, Lyra, and many others. Life was busy, and I couldn't recall the last time I'd looked up and paid attention to the sky or the stars or how many or few there were to see, so this? This experience? It kind of had me shook. It made me think about Bridgette and the ocean, what I said about taking things for granted. I'd been taking the stars, the beautiful sky, for granted.

I was knee deep in that revelation when I felt her grab my hand and squeeze it. When I looked over at her, she was still staring at the ceiling, but now there was a smile on her face, the kind of smile I wore as a kid when my mom would surprise us with candy or ice cream. It was an innocent smile, a pure smile. And in response, I turned my attention back to the ceiling, and I smiled, too.

Bridgette

"Aye! Aye! Aaaaaye! Come on, Nolan! Get it!" I shouted over the sounds of *Bounce, Rock, Skate, Roll*. The crowd in the skating rink was sparse, which was a good thing since poor Nolan was skating like a newborn baby. And yes, I know newborn babies can't walk, let alone skate. My point, exactly.

"When was the last time you skated?" Nolan shouted, as he fought to keep his balance. "This morning? Did you learn to skate in the womb or something?"

I chuckled as I skated around him. He grabbed my arm to keep from falling, almost making me fall. "Um, I think it's been three or four years since I last skated. And I didn't learn until I was an adult. When I first moved out here, I dated this guy who loved to skate. He taught me how, and we'd go skating every Saturday night. I can't believe you never learned how."

"I can ride the shit out of a bike, though. Best believe that."

"Shit, so can I! *And*...I can skate." I turned around, skated backwards for a few feet, and wagged my tongue at him.

"Damn show-off..."

I laughed. "This was your idea, Nole!"

"Hell, I thought it'd be easy to learn."

"It is!" I said, taking off and doing a quick lap around the rink. I was bouncing to the music when I made it back to his side.

Lifting a brow, he said, "I mean this in the most respectful way, so I hope you take it like that. Fuck you."

I laughed so hard, I almost passed out. Then I took his hand. "Come on. Let me teach you. It's all about balancing yourself. To start out, you need to relax and keep your head straight. Don't look at your feet, and just take small steps."

"I feel like I need a fucking helmet," he muttered.

"I got you. I'm not gonna let you fall."

"You promise?" he asked sincerely.

Leaning in and pressing a kiss to his lips, I nodded. "Yeah. I got you."

There was something in his eyes. Relief, maybe, like he'd needed to hear those words. He followed my directions, moving from tiny steps to a decent scissor kick and was gliding before the night was over. Shit, he could almost keep up with me, but got a little too cocky and nearly busted his ass.

We laughed and skated and had such a good time. It felt like we were a couple of teenagers with no worries or responsibilities. And I loved every minute of it.

14

Nolan

"I can't believe you jumped at that one scene!" she said, through a giggle.

"They don't call them jump scares for nothing, Bridgette. I mean, damn, the motherfucker just appeared out of nowhere with that shit hanging off his face. What was I supposed to do? Play it cool, act like that was some normal shit?" I replied, as I followed her up the stairs to her second-floor apartment.

"No, but did you have to jump straight to your feet? I thought you were about to run up out of there!"

"See, now you're exaggerating."

"No, I'm not! I was like, 'Am I gonna have to take an Uber home or something?' And *you* picked the movie out! I wanted to see that new Denzel flick."

"Naw, something is wrong with your ass to just sit there and not flinch."

She fell out laughing then, leaning her head against her door and clutching her stomach, and although she was making fun of my ass, she looked so gorgeous that all I could do was stand there and smile at her.

As her laughter died down, she stuck the key in the lock, tossed me a glance over her shoulder, and said, "Well, thank you for another wonderful night out, with your scary ass."

"It was my pleasure."

She finally turned back around to look at me, key in hand, tilted her head to the side, and upon seeing the expression on my face, said, "What?"

"I love your laugh."

Her smile brightened. "You do?"

"Mm-hmm, and your smile."

"Thank you, Nolan."

"You're welcome."

We stared at each other for a moment before I moved in to kiss her, felt her wrap her arms around my neck, and moved forward until her back was against the door. She wrapped a leg around my waist and I fucking lost it, transforming what was supposed to be a simple good night kiss into virtual foreplay. This woman tasted and felt so good to me, like a damn dream come true, and I guess that's kind of what she was. After all the months of me wanting to know her, wanting to be with her, she was here, and damn if this didn't feel...*right*.

Her phone began to ring, but she didn't miss a beat, pulling me closer to her and returning the kiss, our tongues playing a game of tag. Her phone stopped and mine started. Then mine stopped and both our phones started ringing at the same time.

I released her, and said, "Shit," under my breath while she groaned loudly. We both checked our voicemail messages, looked at each other, and almost simultaneously said, "Jo's in labor!"

Bridgette

Nolan and I rode to the hospital together and arrived in the Labor and Delivery waiting area with our hands clasped and big smiles on our faces, despite the fact that my newest goddaughter had lousy timing. The first face I saw and recognized was that of one of Jo's and South's bodyguards—Oba. The second familiar face was one which mirrored that of the man who held my hand—his twin, Neil. The first time I saw the two of them in the same room, I wondered if they used to play tricks on people when they were young, because when I say they were identical, I mean *identical*. If Neil was a little better kempt, didn't have the wild beard he'd recently grown, they would be indistinguishable. That and their style. Nolan was the type of man who'd never be caught dead without looking his best while Neil's uniform of choice was hoodies, t-shirts, and jeans, but like I said before, he was just as fine as the rest of the male McClains.

"Hey, is Ev back there with Jo? She had the baby yet?" Nolan asked, as we approached Neil.

Looking up from the cell phone in his hand that was holding his attention, Neil frowned at Nolan, let his eyes slide to me, and then down to our joined hands, before fixing them on his twin again. "The fuck y'all got going on?" was how he chose to answer. "This—y'all? Really?"

Nolan sighed. *"Where's Everett, Neil?"*

"Shit, my bad. Yeah...uh, he's back in the room with Jo. I don't know if the baby is here yet or not. Just know she's in labor and fully dilated or something like that."

"Oh, wow! Little Mama will be here any second!" I nearly squealed. "Where's Nat? With Ms. Sherry?"

Neil stared at me for a moment. "Uh, yeah. She's gonna bring her up here after the baby gets here so she can meet her and stuff. Ella's on her way, too."

I grinned and squeezed Nolan's hand. "Good! I can't wait to see the baby!"

Nolan smiled at me as he gestured to a couple of empty seats located in front of where Neil sat. "Me either. Ev's been so excited about this new baby, you'd think it was his first."

"Yeah, he's definitely been hyped up about this little one," Neil agreed.

"Hey, Oba," I greeted the behemoth sitting a few seats over from Neil.

"'Sup, Bridgette. Guess you'll be posting about the baby for Jo, huh?" Oba replied.

I nodded. "That's what she pays me for."

"I forgot you're her assistant. How are you gonna handle those duties once *Floetic Lustice* hits theaters and you become a breakout star?" Nolan asked, turning in his chair to face me.

I rolled my eyes. "Honey is the star. I'm the sidekick. Ain't nobody checking for sidekicks."

He shook his head. "No, you're the standout. Every time you get in front of the camera, *you're* the star, Bridgette. The dailies don't lie. When you're on screen, all I can see is you."

Lowering my voice and my eyelids, I said, "Don't you think you might be a little biased?"

He shrugged as he leaned in and gave me a peck on my lips. "Hmm, maybe? But it's the truth. I've been a film buff all my life, studied film in college, have probably watched thousands of movies. Your talent is rare and natural. I don't even think you try to steal scenes, you just *do*."

I gave him a wink and a little kiss on the cheek. "Well, thank you, Mr. McClain."

"You are more than welcome."

"Okay, time out, time out!" Neil nearly shouted, pulling my attention from his brother to him. He was sitting up straight in the seat he'd been leaning forward in, making a letter "T" with his hands. "What is going on here? I know Ev said something about you liking her that day at your house and you got all sensitive about me talking to her, but is this for real, Nole, or is it some kind of experiment? You tryna see if you like Afro-pussy or something?"

Nolan shook his head as he chuckled bitterly. "Neil, do not start this shit with me in this hospital. If you do, your ass is gonna wake up in one of these rooms in traction from me whooping your ass."

"Naw, man...listen! I'm confused. You been on that Svetlana crack for like what? Nine, ten years straight? And now you're with—and I mean no offense to you, my sister—the most African American woman you could find. I mean, she ain't even really light-skinned, don't have none of that mixed hair, got black features and shit. She ain't even starter black like a damn Mariah Carey or Zendaya or somebody. She looks like a regular black woman. I'm fuckin' flabbergasted!"

"Neil, would you shut the fuck up?"

"Okay, answer me this: is this for real or are you just trying to see if black pussy is still good? For the record, it is."

"How the hell would your no-pussy-getting-ass know?" Nolan countered.

"Fuck you, bitch!"

"If I'm a bitch, I'm a pussy-getting bitch!"

"Hey, hey! Would you two not do this here? Goodness!" I cut in.

"Sorry," they both muttered in their identical voices. While watching them interact was already like a scene from some strange M. Night Shyamalan movie, watching them argue was akin to viewing a Shakespearean tragedy. It was just plain sad.

And since Nolan looked like he was two clicks from turning the waiting area into a wrestling ring, I decided to speak up. "Since you just have to know, Neil, it's real. *Believe me.* It's very real and I'm loving every minute of it."

Neil looked at me as if he was trying to see through me to detect if I was lying, but I wasn't. Yes, I was trying to imply with my words that more was going on between us than a few dates, but honestly, those few dates had been wonderful. Spending time with Nolan had been wonderful. Working with him had been the best experience I'd ever had as an actress. So no, I wasn't lying, and once Neil confirmed that in his mind, he nodded and held up both his hands.

"Hey, I'm glad you two are good together. Congrats, bro," he said.

Nolan mumbled, "Whatever, Neil."

Before either of them could say another word, Big South appeared in the waiting area wearing a set of hospital-issued scrubs that were floods on his tree-tall ass and a big smile. "Our baby girl is here!" he shouted.

*****

"You are beautiful, you know that? But I'm wondering how you could possibly be this tiny when your mom tried to put every rib joint in town out of business over the last nine months. Or not quite nine months, because you're a little early, aren't you? We're gonna have to work on your timing, sister, because you kind of, sort of cockblocked Teetee Bridgette today. Yes, you diiiiiid," I cooed at the gorgeous little brown-skinned girl. Yeah, she looked like a little wet rat, as did all newborns, but she was a pretty little wet rat.

Jo's eyes ballooned as they darted from where I sat next to her bed cradling the baby in my arms to the closed door that Big South, Neil, and Nolan had exited through when they all decided they needed some coffee. Chink was still standing guard outside Jo's room while Oba stood—or rather sat—guard in the waiting area. Big South did not play about his family's safety!

"Don't say cockblocked in front of my baby, and um…you and Nolan done started screwing?" she asked, in a hushed tone.

"So you can say screwing but I can't say cockblocked?"

"You said it again!"

"Really, bish?"

"Are y'all fucking?"

"You just said fucking!"

"Bridgette! In your famous words: spill the tea!"

"I'm trying to, but you are policing my words and that makes it hard to—"

"Ho', if you don't tell me what happened before those men come back in here!"

"Damn, okay! Little bossy ass! So we went to the movies and he drove me home and at my door, we kissed, and when I say we kissed I mean, we *kissed*. Like we was damn near foreplaying until South started blowing our phones up."

"For real?!" she shrieked, making her own sleeping baby flinch.

"Dang, y'all are moving fast. You've been on what now? Five dates?"

I frowned slightly. "Um, five, six, seven, maybe? I don't know. We spend a lot of time together on set, though."

"But...you're ready to have sex with him already?"

"Jo, I'm thirty damn years old, I lost my virginity a long time ago, and I like to have sex. Plus, you already know Nolan is my type. That's why you keep egging this thing on. So yeah, I'm ready, and I'm not ashamed to admit it. You know me well enough to know that. Ain't nothing changed just because it's a McClain man we're talking about."

"Yeah, I know better. Hell, I don't know why I even asked you that."

"Mm-hmm. So you two settled on the name South chose?"

"We did, because his big ass had a tantrum when I protested. I wanted to name her Eva or Eve or Evan after him, but Lena it is."

"I think it's sweet that he wanted to name her after you, and it fits her, you know?"

"It really does, even though I can't tell who she looks like yet."

"Well, so far I can see that she definitely has your lips and South's nose and coloring. Damn!"

"What?!" Jo shrieked. "Is something wrong? There's something wrong with her?! What is it?!"

"Girl, calm down! There's nothing wrong with her. She just opened her mouth, and I'll be damned if I can't see her tooth gap in her gums."

"Oh, I saw that. This freakin' gap is a dominant trait, evidently. Everett is over the moon about it. He's praying she gets my freckles, too. I'm hoping they miss her like they did Nat."

"Well, either way, she's perfect, a good mixture of you and her daddy. Ain't that right, Lena Joy McClain?"

"Sounds like she's an actress or something, doesn't it?"

I smiled as I kissed her little forehead. "It sounds like she's gonna be a superstar."

The door to the room flew open, and in ran a bundle of energy by the name of Natalie Walker.

"Teetee Bijitt! Is that my new baby?!" she chirped, standing on her tippy toes, trying to see little Lena.

South picked her up to give her a better view, as I said, "It sure is, Nat-Nat."

Nat smiled and then looked up at South. "I love her!"

15

Bridgette

Montana was gorgeous, and the beauty of it made the fact that I had to tear myself away from Jo and Nat and baby Lena to make this work trip less tortuous. I wasn't born to be anyone's mother and I accepted that, but I loved my godbabies and my bestie and hated not being able to kiss little Lena's cheeks whenever the mood hit me.

But Montana? The lodge that would serve as our film location and temporary home for the next four days? Well, I don't think I possess an extensive enough vocabulary to adequately describe the majesty of the mountains that provided a gorgeous backdrop, the open sky full of shades of blue and white, the trees, the clean air, the beautiful modern tents. I'd never been the outdoorsy type, but Montana was purity in geographical form, the most beautiful place I'd ever visited.

We were a small group of ten people rather than a full crew and cast. Honey, Nyles, and I were the only actors to be filmed for this portion of the movie—a girls trip that Brother crashes after he and Jazz have an argument. I only had a few lines, so I was surprised I was assigned my own little luxury tent. The tents at this lodge had wood floors and a wooden frame covered in canvas. Mine housed a queen-sized bed—yes, a real bed—a little settee, and a wooden stove to take the edge off the early April chill that was in the air. I even had my own bathroom—a cute little teepee right next to my tent with an actual functioning toilet and rain-head shower in it, along with a sink. Now, I truly understood the meaning of the word, "glamping."

This place was fabulous!

Nolan's tent was right next to mine, and when I went to check it out, I couldn't help but notice that he had a king-sized bed and that his accommodations were roomier than mine, but I guess being the director came with perks. I couldn't complain, though, because one: my paycheck for this movie was nice. Two: not only was I being paid to be there, but hell, my room was paid for, too. So I was being compensated to be pampered, and if I was lucky, I just might travel from second to third base with Nolan while we were there. Shit, this wasn't nothing but a win-win situation for me.

"You like?" His voice came from behind where I stood staring at the mountains, and instead of startling me, it made me smile.

Spinning around to face him, I said, "Yes. It's ... I've never seen anything so beautiful."

"Really? Haven't you been traveling with Ev and Jo? I thought you went overseas with them last year. Figured you'd seen the best of the best of everything by now."

"I did, but I don't know. This is just a different kind of beautiful. I can't really explain it."

He stared at me for a moment, smiled, and said, "Yeah, I know how you feel. Hey, wanna have dinner with me and the Adamses this evening? Then maybe we can take a walk or something alone afterwards?"

"I'd love to."

Leaning in to kiss my cheek, he softly said, "Good. Now, go get in that makeup chair so we can put in this work."

Something about the way he said that made my yoni twitch, so I grinned at him, and said, "Yes, sir, Mr. Director."

*****

"So you're saying you're in love with him? Love? Really?" I asked, as I wrapped the blanket around my shoulders and shivered a little.

"Cynt, it's not even that chilly out here."

"Uh, *I* wasn't raised in New York. Shit, I put on fur boots and a bubble coat when it hits fifty and it's damn forty out here. Now, answer the question at hand. Are you in love with Brother?"

She sighed as she swept some of her flyaway blond hair out of her face. "Yeah, I think I am."

"Then what the hell are you doing here with me? I know we planned this trip months ago, but if I knew things were that deep with him, I would've been cool with rescheduling. You don't fight with your man and then leave the damn state without fixing things, Jazz."

She dropped her eyes and shook her head. "You're right. What am I doing? I need to talk to Brother right now. I need to let him know how I feel."

"I'm glad to hear that. At least I didn't drive all this way for nothing."

We both turned to see him standing behind where we were seated on the pier overlooking the crystal-clear lake.

"Brother!" she shouted, leaping to her feet and flying into his arms.

"Yeah, baby. It's me."

"Cut!" Nolan commanded. "Damn, that was perfect! Can't believe we got that in one shot. I was afraid we'd miss the sunset. Great job, everyone!"

It sounded like everyone present took a collective sigh. I know I did, because getting that scene done at the right time per Nolan's vision had seemed like an impossibility, but I had to admit, Honey running into Nyles' arms right as the sun began to set made for a beautiful shot. We all knew it would and were on board with Nolan but weren't sure if we could make it happen. I was so happy we did.

As I stood and began making my way to my tent, since my work was done for the day, Nolan stepped up beside me, and whispered, "You killed it just like I knew you would. That was phenomenal."

Cheesing like I'd never received a compliment before in my

entire life, I replied, "Thanks, Mr. McClain. See you at dinner."
  "Looking forward to it."

"She kept coming to my shows, sitting front and center, looking like
the answer to a dream I didn't even know I'd had. Tall, pretty as
hell, and her eyes? They hypnotized the shit out of me. She didn't
just stand out in the crowd, she made the whole damn crowd
disappear. One look, and I knew she was mine, that I was made to
love her." After he finished his statement, Nyles Adams grabbed his
wife's hand and kissed it. Then he added, "Damn, I love this
woman."

"You know, I have a whole Spotify playlist of your poetry, but I
don't think any of it is as beautiful as what you just said," I declared,
my hand resting on my chest. Turning to his gorgeous wife, I asked,
"Does he always talk like this? I don't know how you can take it!"

She grinned as she leaned in close to him. "I'm used to it now, but
I'm still his biggest fan. I try not to miss any of his shows, but that's
hard with managing my boutiques and taking care of our little boy."

"But," Nyles cut in, "we have a nanny, so my queen is still
usually front and center when I hit the stage, and projects like this
where we can work together help a lot. When I first started getting
approached for acting gigs, I wasn't sure how we'd work it out, but
we're doing it."

"Well, I'm glad you agreed to be a part of *this* movie. I can
remember when you first got popular back home in Houston and
some of my old friends there told me about you. I finally got a
chance to check you out and you blew me away. Your stage
presence was ridiculous, and I knew right then if I ever made this
movie-making dream a reality, I wanted you to be a part of it,"
Nolan said.

"Thanks, man. I'm glad to be working with you," Nyles replied.

"Hey, did your son come to LA with you?" Nolan asked. "I hope this film isn't keeping y'all away from him."

"Naw, not at all. We don't ever leave our little man behind. Matter of fact, he's here in Montana. He and the nanny got their own tent," Nyles said.

"You paid for it? I would've comped it for you."

"Naw, I got it. Y'all wanna meet him?"

Nolan and I both nodded. I think we were both missing little Lena, because he'd been popping up at South's and Jo's house as much as I had since she cockblocked her way into this world.

Nyles' wife, Trevia, hopped up from the table. "I'll go get him."

While she was gone, Nyles lifted his chin, giving us a little reverse nod. "So...y'all two?"

My eyes widened and shot over to Nolan. If I knew anything, I knew not to define a relationship before the man did. Yeah, I'd laid it on in front of Neil because that was what that situation warranted. This was different, and the way I was feeling Nolan, I couldn't have stomached the embarrassment of him correcting my assumptions about us.

So when he said, "I'm hoping it'll be an 'us two' soon. I'm definitely working toward it," my heart started hopscotching in my chest.

You are already there, baby, I thought.

"Y'all are a good look for each other. Nothing wrong with falling in love and shit, you know?" Nyles said. He had to be the most thuggish poet I'd ever seen. And the finest. Damn!

Yeah, I was all into Nolan, but my ass wasn't blind.

"Yeah, I know," Nolan agreed.

And then time stopped, the stars aligned, and the sun stood still as Trevia Adams made it back to the table holding the hand of the cutest little boy I had ever laid eyes on. Okay, he was in a tie with little Leland, but still, he was an adorable little chocolate kiss with thick hair and long, curly eyelashes, wearing a tiny red Adidas track suit and matching sneakers. He was just beautiful!

I stood, walked over to him, and squatted in front of him in my loose gray jumpsuit and white canvas sneakers. "Hey, there, what's your name?"

"Dallas Trayvon Adams," he said too clearly for a boy his age. Then he held up three little fingers and informed me, "I'm three and I'm tall for my age."

I couldn't help but to chuckle. "And you're very smart and handsome."

He nodded. "Like my daddy."

"Is that right?" I asked, winking up at his mother who was beaming proudly down at him.

"Uh-huh. He's making a moobie." There it was, the only indication he'd given me that he was not, in fact, a grown man in a tiny body.

"Really?! So am I!" I gushed.

"You pretty," he said, then reached out and touched my cheek. This little guy had me grinning so hard my cheeks were stinging.

"Thank you!" I gushed.

"What I tell you about that flirting, lil' man?" Nyles asked, as he left the table and scooped his son up. "Lil' mannish self."

I had to laugh at that. I hadn't heard anyone use the word "mannish" since I was a little girl.

"Well," Nyles began, as he kissed Dallas' cheek, making him giggle, "me and the wife gonna get some time in with this dude before he goes down. It was dope having dinner with y'all. We gotta do this again so y'all can tell us how you two got together."

We all agreed that we'd had a good time and would definitely have to do it again, and then we parted ways.

Nolan and I took that walk he'd mentioned, both of us quiet as we absorbed the sights, sounds, and scents of our surroundings. The grounds were stunning, with gravel trails snaking through lush grass and wooden bridges straddling the lakes. Trees and blue skies hovered overhead, and the air was almost cleansing in its purity. I'd never experienced anything like this. Well, not since I was a little girl in Reola. It was pretty rural and untouched there. I spent plenty of time playing in the woods before my innocence was stolen from me.

"I guess we should be heading to our tents now. Gotta get those last shots in the morning if I'm gonna get the natural lighting I want," Nolan said, breaking the serenity enveloping us.

"But I get to sleep in," I responded, with a wink.

"Yeah, you do, don't you?"

"Mm-hmm. I almost feel guilty for getting this free trip and my own tent for just one scene's work."

He took my hand, clasping it in his. "Don't. I would've wanted you here even if you didn't have a scene."

All I could do was smile.

About ten minutes later, we were at the entrance to my tent, face to face, staring at each other. I liked looking at him, but felt more than a little awkward, and he'd said he needed to turn in early. So I uttered through a sigh, "I enjoyed dinner and our walk."

"Me, too. I hate this night has to end."

"So do I."

He stood there with his eyes on me for a few seconds, then leaned in, kissing me softly and quickly on the lips. I swear electricity—or maybe lack-of-sextricity, because it had been a long while since I'd experienced an orgasm induced by someone other than me—shot down my spine and settled in my core. A simple kiss had never caused that reaction before. It was such an unfamiliar and odd feeling that I had to shut my eyes for a moment to get my bearings. And while they were closed, his lips met mine again, his tongue darting out and swiping my lips. Opening my mouth for him, I slid my arms around his waist, feeling the hardness of his body as he returned my embrace, pulling me close to him. Then his hand was on the back of my head, the other sliding down to my ass. I pressed myself against him, felt the bulge between his legs, and my heart slammed into my rib cage, because...Got. Damn.

He was *blessed.*

He broke away from me abruptly, and I opened my eyes to see the desire in his. I pulled him back to me through no volition of my own, our mouths melding into one as our tongues collided and moans filled the air around us. We kissed for so long that time that when we broke apart, we were both breathing heavily.

"I want you so bad," he practically moaned into my ear as his hand rested on the front of my neck.

"Then take me, baby."

He shook his head. "I don't wanna move too fast. I don't wanna take a chance on ruining this."

"Nolan, I'm thirty, I lost my virginity a long time ago, and I want you. *Right now.* You're not going to ruin anything, and I *want* you to move fast because it's been a long time, I'm horny as hell, and I'm on fire for you. I'm so damn wet, you could drown in me."

"*Got-damn.* You are?"

"Yes, I am. Do you know that sometimes when we're on the phone together, I touch myself because the sound of your voice drives me crazy? You want me? Take me, because I'm here for the taking."

"Shit, baby…uh, Bridgette?"

I leaned in and gently kissed his neck. "Mm-hmm?"

"There's something I need to tell you about me, about— something you need to know before we do this."

I frowned slightly as he dropped his eyes. "Uh, okay?"

He backed away from me a bit, cutting all physical contact between us, and rubbed the back of his head. "I-um-I have this problem. A dysfunction."

Aw, shit. Is he a minute man? It can't be that he has a micro dick because unless he has some damn PVC pipe in his pants, he's packing like a motherfucker. Damn, does he have AIDS? "A dysfunction?"

He nodded and finally lifted his eyes to my face. "An erectile dysfunction."

I dropped my eyes to his crotch. "Um, Nolan? Your dick is hard right now."

"Not that kind of erectile dysfunction."

"What other kind is there?"

"The kind where it takes me longer than normal to ejaculate."

"Oooooh! Well, how long are we talking?"

"I haven't gone less than thirty minutes since I was in high school. My usual is forty-five minutes."

Shit! "For real?"

"Yeah, my doctor says it probably has to do with me being a serial masturbator when I was young. It takes a lot of pressure for me to ejaculate any sooner than that, like the kind of pressure sex can't provide."

I stared at him for a moment and then burst into laughter. I mean, I was doubled over, clutching my stomach with tears in my eyes.

"Damn, that's funny to you?" he asked, sounding more than a little hurt.

"No, no, no! It's just that…" I cleared my throat and wiped my eyes before standing to face him again. "Nolan, I take Prozac, have for years because my childhood was fifty shades of fucked up."

"Uh, thanks for telling me, but what does that have to do with your fucked-up reaction to what I just told you?"

"One of the side-effects of Prozac is delayed orgasm. It takes forever for me to climax, if I climax at all, and most men find it very frustrating. Shit, thirty minutes is child's play to me."

He stared at me for a minute or two before leaning in for another kiss, a long, hot, steamy kiss, and when he came up for air, he growled, "Bridgette?"

"Uh-huh?"

"Can we go inside the tent? Right now?"

"I thought you'd never ask."

We stumbled inside my tent, somehow making our way across the wood floor without running into any of the rustic furniture crowding the space to my bed where I lay on my back with Nolan spreading his body over mine, kissing me as his hand palmed my yoni through my clothes, making the moisture already collecting there morph from a river to a waterfall.

He fumbled with my jumpsuit's drawstring, trying to untie it, until I tore my mouth from his, and mumbled, "It's a one-piece."

"What?" he groaned, as he buried his face in my neck.

"It's a one-piece, baby, a jumpsuit."

"Take it off."

My pussy jumped at the gruffness behind that demand. I watched as he stood from the bed and started shedding his clothes, mesmerized by the body that was slowly revealed as layer after layer fell to the floor. This motherfucker was so damn fine, I forgot I was still dressed, but quickly remembered as he stood over me in his black boxer briefs with an erection that made my mind spin with wild, nasty thoughts. Lifting from the bed, I quickly stripped down to my panties. There was no bra to remove because I wasn't wearing one.

He kissed me again, easing me onto my back on the bed and sliding down my body, licking the seat of my panties and making me lift my ass from the bed and release a low moan. Then he slipped my panties to the side, and I felt the warmth of his tongue as it slid against my clit over and over again. It felt so good that I forgot to worry about how long I knew it would take me to hit my peak. I just let myself relax, my legs flopping to the side, my hand meeting the back of his head as he ate me like my yoni was a porterhouse steak covered in A.1.

Sliding a finger inside me, then two, he continued flicking his tongue against my clit.

"Ooooo, shhhhhhit!" I groaned, as I rocked my hips while holding his head in place.

"Mmmm," he hummed, never taking his mouth off my pussy, his fingers sliding in and out of the slippery mess he'd made.

With my eyes tightly shut, I felt the swelling, swarming, building sensations of an orgasm and began to rock my hips faster to catch it. When the fullness of it hit me, my back left the bed and my head snapped back as I let out a roar like a damn wild animal, followed by, "Damn, Nolan!"

In seconds, his face was hovering over mine, his lips wet with me as he devoured my mouth while rubbing my pulsating yoni with his hand. "See how good you taste?" he asked.

"I can't feel my damn legs," I whined.

"You can't? Wanna stop?" he asked, a deep frown on his face.
"*Hell*, no!"

He chuckled as he stood from the bed and sheathed himself with a condom I didn't know he had. Shit, I had no idea where it even came from. I just knew I wanted him to hurry up and put it on.

When he entered me, I gasped, grabbed his shoulders, and released a hissing sound. "Shit!" I screamed, despite the fact that there was only a canvas flap that served as a door and no real roof. Just the canvas shell, but hell, I couldn't help it.

"Got damn, Bridgette!" he groaned, as he slid in and out of me, grabbing one of my legs and placing it on his shoulder. Then he leaned in and kissed me while twisting one of my nipples hard, like he was trying to twist the motherfucker off...and it hurt so damn good. The things he was doing to me...it was all too much, but at the same time, I wanted more of it. I wanted *all* of it. Whatever he had to give, I was willing to accept, because it felt like pure bliss to me.

"Baby, shit! Damn-it! Fuck!" Nolan grunted. "Motherfucking shit, Bridgette!"

"No, no, no, no—"

He stopped moving, and I opened my tightly shut eyes. "Why'd you stop? Shit, why'd you stop?"

"You said no."

"I was tryna say your name."

"So you don't want me to stop?"

"No! Shit, please don't stop!"

"Okay, baby."

He eased out of me, then back in, smacked my thigh, and we resumed our little cursing match:

"*Got dammit, Nolan!*"

"*Fuck, Bridgette! Shit, baby!*"

"*This motherfucking dick is so good!*"

"*Ohhhhh, fuck!*"

His dick was so good, it had me thinking strictly in Maya Angelou quotes. I mean, my brain was spewing stuff like:

"*I've learned that people will forget what you said, people will forget what you did, but people will never forget how you made them feel.*"

And he was making me feel reeeeal good!

Or: "*When someone shows you who they are, believe them the first time.*"

He was showing me he had some good, long-winded dick!

And: "*I got my own back.*"

But he had this pussy!

I reached up, kissed him as he glided in and out of my saturated yoni, and yelled, "You good-dicked sonovabitch!"

"This pussy...shit!" was his response.

"You know this is your pussy now, don't you? It's yours. Only yours. Can't nobody else have it. Do you understand me?!"

"Oh, damn! You feel good as hell!"

After I was blessed with another orgasm, was bathed in Nolan's sweat, and became damn near paralyzed from the hips down, he let out a grunt, losing his rhythm as he hit his peak before collapsing onto me, and murmuring, "Shit, baby."

16

Nolan

Her skin was so smooth, so soft. The only blemish I could find on her silky brown skin was a scar to the left of her navel. I traced it with my fingertip then dragged my hand down to her thigh, letting it rest there.

"Nolan?" she said softly.

"Yeah?" I answered.

"Are you seeing anyone besides me?"

"No. Don't wanna see anyone else. Are you?"

"No. Nolan?"

"Yeah, baby?"

"Don't start seeing anyone else."

"Like I said, I don't want anyone else. Especially not now."

"Good."

"Bridgette?"

"Yeah?"

"Did you mean what you said about your pussy being mine, or was that just some heat of the moment talk?"

"How would you feel if I said I meant it?"

"I damn sure wouldn't be mad about it. I'd be elated."

"Then I meant it."

"Good. Hey, I got another question for you."

"Okay. What?"

"Did you bring any stilettos with you?"

"Yes."

"Put 'em on, baby."

"Now?"

"Yeah. Now."

"Well, since you said it like that…"

She pulled my face to hers, kissed me, and left the bed, digging in her luggage, unearthing a black pair of shoes with a shiny silver heel, sliding them on, and then standing at the foot of the bed in nothing but them.

"Come here."

Her eyes widened as she stepped closer to me with her bottom lip tucked between her teeth. Grabbing her wrist, I pulled her down to straddle my lap, taking my finger and dragging it from the hollow of her neck between her breasts and then reaching around and smacking both her ass cheeks at the same time, making her jump. "Do you have any damn clue how much you turn me on, how much you've always turned me on since the moment I first laid eyes on you?"

"Why didn't you say something to me?"

"To be honest, you intimidated the shit out of me, and from the time I first met you that Thanksgiving, you were already with Tommy."

"Not really. I mean, we were just getting to know each other back then. And weren't you there with someone?"

"Yeah. Like I said, I don't like being alone."

She smiled and spread her arms wide. "And now you got all this."

After I'd leaned in and dragged my tongue from her neck to her right breast, I said, "Speaking of all this…lift up, baby."

Her eyes flashed as she rose from my lap.

As I lined my dick up with her sex, I said, "You like it when I tell you what to do, Bridgette?"

Closing her eyes, she replied, "Mmmm, yeah. There's something about your voice when you get all directorish. But don't tell me to do no crazy shit."

"I was just gonna tell you to ride this dick. Is that crazy?"

As she eased down on me, she whined, "No…it's…noooot!"

I flicked my tongue against her nipple before taking it in my mouth and nibbling on it as she bounced in my lap until we were both sweaty, exhausted, and thoroughly satisfied.

*****

"Aye, how's the Montana filming going? You getting all them Iñárritu shots you wanted to get done?" Everett asked.

I halted my steps on the pier. "You know who that is?"

"Yeah, nigga. I pay attention to movie shit, too."

"My bad. Yeah, we're done with all the shots that required natural lighting. Got one more scene to do and I think we can get it done tonight. Honey and Adams are so good, it usually only requires a few takes to get what I want."

"Okay, good. You killing this director shit, huh?"

"Man, I'm trying. How's Lena? Jo?"

"Good, good. I mean, we tired because Little Mama love to keep us up, but it's all good."

"That's great, man. Uh, hey...I actually called to ask you something."

"A'ight, what is it?"

I leaned against the railing and peered out at the lake. "You ever notice how beautiful the world is? You know, the sky and the trees? The birds singing. I never noticed how beautiful birds sing. They be all in tune and shit, too. You know, 'tweep-tweep...tweep-tweep.' That shit is wild, man."

"What the fuck?"

"No, listen. I'm just saying...it's good to be alive, Ev. It's just good to be breathing and shit with your heart beating. You ever thought about how your heart just beats all the time on its own?"

"Nigga, are you high? Got-damn, now, Nole. You can't be fucking up, too. I got my hands full with Neil, got him staying here, had to lock my damn liquor up and shit, and I got a new baby. Shit, now!"

"Naw, naw...you know I don't do shit like that. I just...man, life is good, you know?"

"You sound like you done had some good pussy. If you ain't high, that's the only explanation for this existential bullshit you spitting right now."

"Ev…I ain't never experienced anything like I did last night. It was so damn good. So damn good…"

"Nole, is your ass crying?"

I sniffled. "No."

"Yes the-fuck you are! Who'd you fuc—Bridgette? You finally got with Bridgette?!"

"Yeah, man, and I think I'm in love or something. It was the best night of my life. I can't stop thinking about it. I feel like a damn junkie or something."

"Shit, I know that feeling."

"How did you handle it?"

"I married her, and she just had my baby."

I wiped my eyes because some sweat was leaking out of them. "It's too soon to marry her."

"Well, shit, you just keep being with her and fucking her and stuff. Like you been doing with all them Albanian chicks. You know the drill."

"She's different."

"You ate her pussy, didn't you?"

"Yeah, man. And it was—"

"You ain't gotta tell me. She the damn queen of pineapples. She's the one who told Jo about them."

"What?"

"You ever heard Rozay's *Diced Pineapples*?"

"Yeah? Ohhhh!"

"Yep. Look, I know this shit is overwhelming, but you gon' be a'ight. Just keep her by your side, let her know you got her, and what you had last night will be all yours for life."

"Damn, you think?"

"I *know*. Aye, I think I hear the baby. Lemme go see."

"Okay, thanks, Ev."

"No problem, man."

I was making my way to the tents to check on Bridgette when I saw her on the same stone path, walking toward me wearing a long orange dress and white heels, her hair that she usually wore straight and parted down the middle, slicked back into a ponytail. My dick sprung to attention as I involuntarily quickened my strides.

When we were face to face, she smiled, and said, "Glad I ran into you. I was just gonna see if you wanted to have lunch—"

Grabbing her at the back of the neck, I pulled her face down to mine and kissed her, easing my tongue inside her mouth as she moaned. I slid my hand around and gripped her ass, deepening the kiss, and when I pulled away, I dropped down to my haunches, pulled her dress up right there on the path, and slid my hand between her legs.

She opened them with a little stumble while whimpering, "N-Nolan...you wanna go to the t-t-tent?"

I didn't answer her. Shit, I *couldn't* answer her because I'd already slid her little panties out of my way and had my tongue on her clit. She grabbed my head as I lifted her leg, placing it on my shoulder.

"Nolan...shit! Uh, we're gonna get c-caughtttttt!"

"Mm-hmm," I moaned, licking her whole damn split while gripping her ass.

I thought I heard footsteps on the path, then voices, but I didn't stop and soon heard the footsteps retreating. She didn't lie about having delayed orgasms. It took me a few minutes of concentrated work, but after I added my fingers to the mix and kept my tongue working her clit, her planted leg began to shake and she let out a little gurgling, hissing, shriek while death-clutching my head, until the orgasm abated.

When I could tell her breathing was getting back to normal, I stood, kissed her again, and pulled a handkerchief out of my suit coat pocket, wiping my mouth with it. After I shoved it back in my pocket, I said, "Let's go eat."

"Uh, I don't think I can walk," she whined.

"Really?"

"Yeah."

Kissing her once again, I picked her up, wrapping her legs around my waist, and carried her to the pavilion where lunch was being served.

17

Bridgette

"Teetee Bridgette missed her baby. Yes, she did. You got bigger, didn't you? Tryna fill out. Don't you be growing up fast like your sister," I cooed at little Lena, kissing her cheek as I cradled her in my arms.

"How was Teetee Bridgette's trip to Montana? You've been back a week and still haven't filled me in," Jo said, from her seat next to me on her sofa.

"You know what? Your mama never thanked me," I said, my eyes glued to the baby.

"For what?" Jo asked.

"Let's see…just to name a few things? For letting your job-hopping ass room with me when you first moved to LA and for making you go in South's VIP room that night at *The Launch Pad*."

She rolled her eyes. "What does any of that have to do with Montana?"

"Thank me and I'll connect the dots."

Through a sigh, she said, "Thank you, Queen Bridgette."

"You're welcome. Now *I* can thank *you*."

"For what, Bridge?" I was working her nerves and I loved it.

"For connecting me to Nolan via your connection to South, because girlllll, shit!"

Jo turned her whole body to face me, her eyes wide. "Bitch, what happened?!"

"Jo, my dear BFF, that man is ev-ery-thing! I mean, damn! Dick for days and a stroke for years! Shit, I swear I could fall in love with him without really trying. I ain't been back to my apartment since before I left for Montana, because I been at his place in his bed up under his beautiful body. And his damn tongue? Child, it's like he's half iguana or some shit. I ain't never had it like this. I'll hurt a bitch over Nolan Jacob McClain!"

"Damn, you know his middle name?"

"Mm-hmm. Shoe size and driver's license number, too. Hell, I have his STD test results in my email inbox right now and he has mine. Shit, I even had my doctor check to make sure my IUD is in good condition. I'm not playing, sis."

Jo grinned at me. "So, you know I already knew about this, right? About y'all finally 'getting together' in Montana? I was just waiting for you to spill it. But anyway, Nolan called Everett while y'all were still in Montana, and from what Ev says, the feeling is definitely mutual. Nolan is all in! What you put on him?"

"This country-ass, raised on pinto beans and cornbread Reola, Alabama, coochie, that's what! The same thing you put on South. Jo, I will marry that motherfucker, and you know I ain't messed up about marriage unless the man is like a billionaire or something. Shit, he about to make me break my no-babies code, too."

"You need to break that anyway."

"You know I got my reasons for it. Anyway, I'm just so…happy right now. For however long this lasts, I'm gonna enjoy myself *and* enjoy him. Shit, I deserve him and his penis."

She high-fived me. "I know that's right! Oh, is that yours or mine?" she asked, referring to the text message alert that'd just dinged.

I shrugged, because I wasn't about to put that little piece of heaven down to check my phone.

Jo picked up both our phones, and after checking both screens, said, "Someone you got programmed in here as *Roots* says, 'Hey.' Who or what is *Roots*?"

"Nolan," I replied, as I kissed Lena's little hand. To be so young, I could swear she was staring right at me, eyes focused and everything.

"Why you got him in here as *Roots*?"

"Because that's the longest movie I could think of."

"It's a miniseries, not a movie, but it *is* long as hell. I gave up on watching the remake. Too much damn work."

"Exactly. It's looooong, and that directly relates to Nolan."

"Hooker, is he packing like that?! Damn! He is truly his brother's brother then…"

"First of all, he *is* packing like that, but that's not what the name is for."

She just sat there, her eyes on me, eyebrows tented with expectancy.

As I leaned back on the sofa, placing the baby on my chest, I informed her, "Let's just say, he is the antithesis of a minute man. More like an I'm-dripping-wet-in-sweat-legs-numb-fall-into-an-exhaustion-induced-coma-afterwards man. Shit, I don't think I need the gym anymore now that I got him. He is long-winded as hell…and I love it, because it's thirty to forty-five minutes of exquisite dick."

"Thirty-to-forty-five minutes? Every time?! Shit! No wonder you're wearing a ponytail. You done sweated that perm out, ain't you?"

"Yep. But shit, I'll do a big chop before I give that up!"

"Okay?!" Jo agreed, high-fiving me again.

Little Lena started rooting around my chest, and I moved to hand her to Jo. "Ut! I ain't got nothing for you, little bit. Let me give you to your kitchen."

"I would be insulted about being called a kitchen, but…"

As she started pulling titties out, I grabbed my phone from beside her and returned Nolan's text with: *Hey yourself.*

Roots: *You having lunch with me today? I miss you on set.*

Me: *How can you miss me when you just saw me this morning?*

Roots: *Busted. I actually just miss your pussy.*

Me: *LMAO! Glad to know we're on the same page, because all I see when I see you is your penis.*

Roots: *Good, because what I meant by having lunch was having sex. Sex is lunch in Nolanese.*

Me: *Nolanese? Is that a new language?*

Roots: *Yeah. A romantic language boasting only a few words: Bridgette's pussy, Bridgette's ass, sexy Bridgette, wet Bridgette, Bridgette in my bed. Stuff like that.*

Me: *Those are phrases, not words.*

Roots: *It's my language. I make the rules. Come have lunchsex with me, baby. You're on the menu and I'm hungry as hell.*

Shit! Me: *Okay, I guess you twisted my arm. Let me finish up here at Jo's and I'll meet you at the studio.*

Roots: *Bridgette's clit (That's "thank you" in Nolanese)*
Me: *Wow*

"I ain't paying you to sit over there and grin while texting my brother-in-law," Jo said, as little Lena drained her dry.

"I'ma take your old funky pictures and put them on IG, you damn task master. You just concentrate on being a soda fountain and leave me alone. Now you see how all those rib joints and chicken joints and pizza parlors and food trucks and taco stands and vending machines felt when you were pregnant, huh?"

"Such a hateful heifer. I can't stand your ass..."

As I hopped up and began snapping photos of the three strollers and two car seats Jo had recently received as gifts for the baby, I had to shake my head. The gifts were from big-name companies like Gucci and Steve Madden and even fucking Cosmo magazine had sent a layette set. What kind of damn sense did it make to gift a billionaire's baby with this much shit? The world was so damn backwards.

Nolan

Life was good. Shit, it was *great*. Filming was going well. The club was basically running itself, because I was too busy with the movie to really manage it and it hadn't burned down yet. And the best thing about my life?

Bridgette.

These two weeks since getting back from Montana, we'd damn near been joined at the hip, spending nearly every day together on set even if she wasn't scheduled to film, eating lunch together, having dinner together, her sleeping in my bed after we wore each other out with the best damn sex I'd ever had. Us laughing and talking, watching TV or movies, or not doing shit but being together. Damn, it felt good. It felt *right*. It felt like she was mine. I'd never had a *mine* before, never wanted one before, but now? Bridgette was the answer to everything for me. She was just...*it*.

"That crazy wench is gonna get caught, lurking around the damn crime scene looking all murdererish. Who does that? I swear these killers be dumb as hell," she cracked from her seat next to me in my bed in nothing but one of my t-shirts and her panties.

She basically lived with me now, and I loved that shit. I could just roll over and get it when the mood hit me. And the mood was always hitting me.

Matter of fact...

I slid my hand between her thighs. "I don't know why you watch this shit. The title alone is nuts. *Murder Comes to Town?* The fuck?"

"This is educational, Nole. If you ever need to commit a murder, you'll know what *not* to do."

"You're crazy as hell, you know that? And kinda scary."

She turned to look at me. "You scared of me? I mean, I know you like to scream like a girl when we watch horror movies, but..."

"You just can't let shit go, can you?"

"Admit it, you're a big-old scaredy cat!"

"I ain't scared of this pussy, though," I said, as I slipped my hand inside her panties.

"You just gonna play with it like that while I'm tryna see if they gonna catch this fool? Not even gonna ask permission first?"

"I thought it was mine. I gotta get permission to play with something that's mine, Bridge?"

As she slid down in the bed and opened her legs in response to the finger I'd just eased inside her, she whimpered, "Oooooo, no you dooooon't."

"That's what I thought."

18

Bridgette

"I'm not gonna lie, when I took over as director, I almost shit myself," Nolan said, garnering a room full of laughs. "But y'all are a great cast and crew. You kept working without missing a beat, embraced me as a director even though this was my first crack at it. Didn't bail on the project when I know most of y'all agreed to work on it because Lazarus Holmes was brought on as director. I appreciate the loyalty and all the hard work, and I believe we have a hit on our hands."

Hoots and applause filled the first floor of *Second Avenue.*

"I'ma shut up so we can get this party started—"

"Thank God, with your long-winded ass!" South quipped from his seat at our table.

Everyone laughed, and Nolan said into the microphone, "I'm thirty-six years old, and he still treats me like a kid, but I gotta thank him, too, for making this happen."

"Ain't nothing, man," South said, and the crowd awww'd in response.

"Anyway," Nolan continued, "I just wanna say that over these eight weeks of filming, this hasn't felt like a job. It feels like we've built a family, and I hope to work with you guys again in the future. So, with that said, I want you all to have a good time. You deserve it!"

As Nolan left the stage, the DJ cranked the music up and the *Floetic Lustice* wrap party was in full swing. I was smiling as I watched him weave his way through the crowd back to our table, where we'd been joined by Jo—who was so glad to be out of the house and childless, she looked like she was a second from jumping on the table and twerking—returning from the restroom to her seat next to her hubby. Neil was there, too, probably sneaking a drink since he was on the Big South rehabilitation plan. Sage and her man were out on the dancefloor along with most of the cast and crew. A lot of Nolan's friends were there, too. Mostly guys he'd known since college, all businessmen, all serious-looking with tiny women on their arms.

"You did good, baby," I said, once he'd slid into the chair closest to mine and given me a peck on my cheek."

"You think? I was almost as nervous as I used to be when I'd try to talk to you."

"I don't know why I made you nervous, Nole."

"Have you seen your legs and booty?"

I rolled my eyes. "You need to quit."

"She's right, man. Good job all around. I'm proud of you, little brother," South said.

"You know that means a lot coming from you. Thanks for getting on board with this vision of mine and putting your money in it. This was my dream, and like you always do, you made it come true," Nolan replied earnestly.

"Awww, y'all are so sweet," Jo gushed. "With that said, let's hit the floor, baby." She hopped up and basically dragged a chuckling Big South behind her.

"Yes, ma'am," he said.

"Well, I need the restroom. Be back." After kissing Nolan, I left our table and navigated my way toward the ladies' room, was almost there when I crossed paths with Nolan's friend, Mike, who was with another of Nolan's friends. I think his name was Rourke or something like that.

"Hey! Congrats on y'all wrapping up the film. Nole says you're a superstar! Can't wait to see you in action at the premiere," Mike said.

"Yeah, congrats, baby!" That was Rourke.

My smile faltered, and I had to wonder if this dude just called everyone baby. Otherwise, what the fuck? "Uh, thanks. And thanks for coming out to help us celebrate."

"Oh, most definitely. You know we had to come out and support our guy," Mike said.

Then we all just stood there, and it felt hella awkward, so I asked, "Is your fiancée here with you tonight, Mike? I'll have to make sure I find her and say hello."

"Naw, she didn't come. Hey, I'ma just cut to the chase. No sense in bullshitting. How much for me and Rourke?"

"How much for what?" I asked, with a grin on my face. Mike was a clown. I remembered that from his party, so I figured this was going to be a dig at Nolan. Like, Nolan was paying me to pretend to be his girl or something.

"To fuck," Rourke spoke up. "When you're done with Nole, I mean. He got you all night?"

"Naw, he been with her for a minute now. Guess he's really enjoying her," Mike informed him.

"I bet you expensive as hell!" Rourke damn near yelled.

"Sho' you right! You gotta pay top dollar to even glance at the black girls from what I hear," Mike agreed.

"What the fuck are y'all talking about?" I asked, my hands balling into fists. "You think I'm some damn hooker?!"

"I mean, you *are* with Nole, so…"

"I ain't no got-damn hooker, and if I *did* sell pussy, I wouldn't sell it to you two baby dick-having motherfuckers! I can't believe this shit!"

If they had a rebuttal, I didn't hear it because I turned on my heels and stomped back to our table and right in front of Jo and Big South, hissed, "Nolan, I'm ready to go."

"Ready to go? The party just started, baby," Nolan said, with a confused look on his face. "I thought you were looking forward to this."

"Fuck it. I'll take a Lyft," I mumbled, as I grabbed my purse from the table.

"Bridge, what happened?" Jo asked knowingly.

"Nothing, except Nolan's friends seem to think I'm a fucking prostitute. Two of them just tried to pay me to fuck them, to fuck both of them, *at the same time*, because evidently that's how Nolan gets down."

"What?!" Nolan, Jo, and South all shrieked at the same time.

"Who the fuck said that?!" Nolan yelled, hopping up from his seat.

"Who said you pay for pussy?" I asked. "Mike and Rourke."

Nolan took off before I could say another word, followed by South, and I took that opportunity to make my exit with Jo on my heels.

"Bridge, wait!"

With my head in my phone, trying to secure a ride, I kept walking, only stopping once I was outside and could finally breathe again. It'd felt like steam was encasing my face, thick steam. And my heart was galloping out of control.

"Bridgette!" Jo called, finally catching up with me. "Damn, I just had a baby! You gotta slow down." Chink was right behind her, struggling to keep up.

"I'm fine, Jo. Go back inside."

"No, you're not. You look like you're about to fuck someone up. Come back inside. Let me and Everett take you home."

"No, I'm good."

"What's going on?! Whose ass we need to kick?!" Sage asked, as she hurried toward us. "I saw you run up outta there like you had an appointment to whoop a bitch!"

"Nothing is going on other than Nolan got his friends thinking they can pay me for pussy," I informed her.

"What?! Nolan? Nerdy-ass looking Nolan? I mean he fine, but them suits and slacks...Nolan?! For real?"

"Yes, Sage. Fucking Nolan! See, that's what I get for caring about a motherfucker. I let this shit move too fast. I done damn near moved in with this asshole. Fuck me!"

"Bridgette!" That was Nolan and my cue to start walking, because fuck this *and* him.

As I started walking to, I don't know, *somewhere*, I said, "Go fuck yourself, Nolan, fuck your whole self!"

"You just gonna run off without letting me explain? That's fucked up!"

I kept walking. "So is having someone ask how much I charge to let them fuck! What kind of shit is that?"

"The kind of shit that got them kicked out of my club and my life and woulda got their asses kicked if Ev hadn't stopped me."

Shaking my head, I kept walking. "Whatever."

"Bridgette, got-dammit, stop and let me explain this shit!"

There was that take-charge director voice again, the one that made my coochie cream, and as bad as I wanted to defy it, I couldn't. At least not totally. I turned to face him, arched an eyebrow, and assented. "Fine, you can explain while you take me home, to *my* place."

"Thank you," he said, as he tried to cup my elbow.

I snatched away from him. "Don't touch me."

He sighed. "All right, baby. Just come on."

"First, let me say I'm sorry Mike and Rourke came at you like that. They'll be dealt with."

I kept my eyes focused on the scene outside his windshield. We were on my complex's parking lot, Nolan having decided to wait until we got there to begin his little explanation. I didn't respond, because it didn't take much for me to shut down, a side effect of my fucked-up childhood, and I was in deep shut-down mode at that moment.

"Second, I've never paid a woman for sex in my life."

"Humph," I said.

"Baby, I haven't!"

"So they made that shit up, Nolan? Really?" Yeah, I'd turned the power back on in response to the stupid shit he was saying.

"They're talking about *The Gallery*, but they got shit all twisted up. They could never get in there so they're making assumptions about how it works."

I twisted around in my seat and narrowed my eyes at him. "What the hell are you talking about? What damn gallery? And what does an art gallery have to do with—"

"It's not an art gallery, it's a club. An exclusive club where people who can afford membership go to find women."

Nolan

She stared at me, eyes wide as she shook her head. "A-a brothel?"

"No, no, not a brothel. A club, like a lodge or something like that. You pay for access to the women, but access doesn't guarantee sex."

"What kind of women?"

"All kinds of women. Foreign women."

"Russian women?"

"Yes."

"That's how you met the women you used to date? At this club?"

"Yes."

"You had sex with these women, right?"

"I went on dates with them, spent time with them, and yeah…I had sex with them, but I never gave money to any of them."

"That's how brothels work, Nolan. You pay the pimp or madam, not the hooker."

"They're not hookers! It's not a brothel! It-it's a dating service, a high-end dating service. People go there to match up with someone they can spend time with, maybe even marry."

"But people like your asshole friends *think* it's a brothel."

"They—yeah, I guess they do."

"Did you pass these women around to your friends or something? What made them think they could have me? They think I'm from this gallery?"

"I guess they assumed I found you there, but no...I didn't pass anyone around. They used to ask me about some of the women I was with after I stopped seeing them, tell me how they wanted them, and I'd tell them to go for it because I didn't care...and I didn't, but I also knew they didn't have the bank account to entertain them."

"When's the last time you were at *The Gallery*?"

"A couple of weeks before we started filming."

"When's the last time you were with a woman other than me?"

"Same amount of time, a couple of weeks before we started filming."

We were both quiet as I guess she tried to absorb what I'd told her and I tried to figure out how to hold onto her.

Finally, I said, "Look, I'm not proud of this, Bridgette, and I've done a lot of fucked-up things, but I've never paid for pussy, at least not directly, and I never gave Mike and Rourke the impression that you were a prostitute. I care about you and I don't want what we have to end, so say the word. Tell me what I need to do to make this right."

Her eyes searched the windshield, then locked with mine. "Do you still belong to this...club?"

"Well, yeah. Membership dues are paid annually. I'm paid up until next January, but I'll cancel my membership. I don't need it anymore."

"Take me there."

"What?"

"Take me to *The Gallery*. I want to see it."

"Uh, Bridge—"

"Can you bring guests?"

"Yeah..."

"Then let's go. Now."

"And do what?"

"Do you want me, Nolan?"

"You know I do."

"Then take me there. Otherwise, I'm climbing out of this car and out of your damn life."

I scratched my forehead. "We can't just pop up. There are rules. I'd need to call and let them know I'm coming."

"Then call."

I stared at her, could see that she was serious, and then grabbed my phone from its holder on the dashboard, and made the call.

*****

Once upon a time, the familiarity of the sights, sounds, and smells of that place excited me. But this time, it felt wrong and awkward as hell to be stepping through the big metal door with Bridgette by my side.

"I have passed by this building a million times. I thought it was just some random warehouse, not...*this*," Bridgette said, her eyes inspecting the dark entryway.

I didn't respond, because the only thought in my mind was of grabbing her hand and leaving, but if we left, I might lose her. Shit, if we stayed, I might lose her. I couldn't win.

"McClain! Glad you actually made it this time. And with a lovely guest," Heather, a tall, waifish blond, greeted me and then turned her attention to Bridgette. "I'm Heather, your hostess, and I'd better get you tagged right now before someone tries to steal you from McClain here."

"Tagged?" Bridgette said, her eyes jumping from Heather to me. "What the hell?"

Before I could explain, Heather lifted the bright orange bracelet. "With this on your arm, everyone will know you're a guest and not, um, available."

"Where's his? He ain't available either," Bridgette asked, a hand on her hip.

"Uh, there are no males to choose from here, baby. Only women," I explained.

"Yes, the men are at *The Exhibition*. I can get you in touch with their hostess if you're interested in a membership," Heather directed at Bridgette.

I was just about to say, "Hell no she ain't interested," but Bridgette beat me to it.

"Naw, I'm good. No exhibitions for me," she muttered, with her lips curled in a snarl.

I tried to convince myself that I wasn't going to end up alone by the time this night was over as we followed Heather to my regular room where two armchairs, a small table, a glass of champagne, and two glasses were the only things occupying the small space other than the black-curtain covering one wall and a control panel on another wall. But my positive thoughts weren't reaching my heart. This was bad, and I almost felt like throwing the hell up.

After we'd taken our seats and Heather had left, I asked, "You want some champagne?" because I couldn't think of anything else to say.

She gave me a look, and I mumbled, "Never mind."

"So now what?" she queried.

I sighed. "Baby, can we please—"

"No. Now what happens?"

I closed my eyes for a second, then stood and pressed a button on the control panel. The curtains before us separated to reveal a brunette sitting on the other side of the glass at her own table, sipping her own champagne. She smiled at us and nodded.

"She can see us?" Bridgette whispered.

"Yeah, she can see us, but she can't hear us."

"Damn, that's a nice dress she got on," Bridgette said, then shook her head. "So we just sit here and stare at each other?"

"No...if-usually, like before you, if I liked what I saw and wanted to get to know her, I'd use the intercom to invite her to join me."

Her eyes searched the room until they bumped into the intercom integrated with the control panel. "And if you didn't want to get to know them?"

I'd hit the button and close the curtain and she'd know to leave. Then another woman would take her place. I'd wait a few minutes and open the curtains again."

"So, you hold all the power? *Men* hold all the power here?"

"No, baby. You're sitting on this side of the window, too. Right now, you got just as much power as I do."

Her eyes were glued to me for a full three or four minutes, then she covered her face with her hands. "Oh my God, Nolan. This is just..."

"Wrong. I know. I realize that now. Nothing about this feels right anymore."

"It's prostitution. No matter how you try to dress it up, it's prostitution. These women are being pimped!"

"Baby...I'm sorry, but this is my past, an embarrassing past. I don't do this anymore."

"You really ain't shit, you know that? You paying to belong to this club is tantamount to you paying for pussy. You. Ain't. Shit!" she shouted.

"I know I'm not. I'm fucked up! *This* is fucked up, but this is my damn truth. It's fucking pathetic and I know it. The smartest McClain is really the dumbest McClain. I'd come here, pick a woman, mess with her for a while, and move on to the next. Always looking, searching for something I was only gonna find in you. I know that now. What I needed, what I always wanted, is you. I care about you, baby, have damn near since the day I met you. I have wanted you for just as long and-and shit, now that I got you, I don't wanna lose you. I am sorry, Bridgette. *I am.* You're right. I was basically paying for pussy, but I never told anyone I found you here. I would never do that. I respect you. I don't wanna do anything but protect you. Hell, I think I love you. Never been in love before, but that's gotta be what this is, because I think I might die if I lose you, and I'm not playing. My fucking heart hurts right now just from the possibility of losing you."

We were both silent for a couple of minutes, until she said, "Close the got-damn curtain."

Her voice told me that pouring my heart out had no impact on her, so I basically stood and shuffled over to the wall, hit the button, and when I turned around, found that Bridgette was on her feet right behind me, glaring at me.

"Baby, please—" I started, but she cut me off.

"Shut. Up," she ordered, then dropped to a squat in front of me. The next thing I knew, she was unfastening my belt and unzipping my pants and pulling them and my underwear down and putting me in her mouth.

"Wait-what-shit!" I stammered, happy and scared and hard as a damn rock all at the same time. "Baby—"

Popping me out of her mouth, she said, "Didn't I tell you to shut up?" Then she went back to work.

"Got-damnnnn! My bad, baby!"

"One more word and I'ma stop."

I quickly glued my mouth shut and tried not to fall, because...shit!

She slurped and sucked, swirling her tongue around me and making my damn legs vibrate. It didn't take me thirty minutes. Shit, I don't even think it took five minutes for me to explode, and as I stood there slumped against the wall, trying to catch my breath and waiting for the feeling to return to my legs, she hopped to her feet and swiped at her mouth.

"I don't know what you're gonna have to do, because it seems that all of your friends are ass wipes—Lazarus, Mike, Rourke—but better not another friend of yours call me a whore. I can stand being called a bitch before I can take being called a whore, but they better not call me a bitch, either," she said.

I nodded, reaching down to pull my underwear back up. "It'll never happen again. I promise."

"And if you ever step foot in here again, it's over between us."

"I won't."

"When we leave this room, you're cancelling your membership. Tonight."

"No problem."

"One last thing."

"Anything."

"Where are the black women? They don't have any black women here?"

"Upstairs. Top floor."

"Why didn't you ever get with them? Didn't you say all the women here are foreign? Why didn't you want a foreign sister?"

"Couldn't afford it. You gotta pay top dollar to get up there. Black and Latino women, or exotic women as they're labeled, are the most expensive to gain access to."

"Well, I can't believe that, the way folks shit on us brown women."

"That might be true outside these walls, but in here? Not so. The black women here come from famous lineages, like Zulu and Yoruban women. Women from purely African bloodlines. There are some men who are willing to pay a lot for a woman who's purely African. I heard one guy say sleeping with one of those women was like sleeping with the cradle of the earth. To men like him, Russian women and any other white women, are a dime a dozen. That's why she tagged you so quickly, so you wouldn't get attacked down here and then I'd have to go to jail for fucking some of these thirsty men—or women—up."

"So, the other club members are in rooms like these?"

"Yeah."

"This is some sick shit."

"I know. I…I'm ashamed as hell right now. And I just…"

"But you having all this power here and telling me I had the same power kinda turned me on, so that's why I did what I just did."

"Oh…"

"Nolan, listen." She sighed, moving closer to me and leaning against my body. "You said this is your past and I believe you. Your friends blindsided me with that mess, and I just…I don't want to be hurt or made a fool of, because I care about you, too."

"Then believe that you're the reason I stopped coming here and you're the reason I'm never coming back. Trust me."

"I do. Just don't make me regret it."

"I won't, baby."

19

Nolan

A week had passed since Mike and Rourke almost messed my world completely up, and I'd been spending every second I wasn't in the editing bay with Danny Steele, an editing genius who I knew from film school, with Bridgette—holding her, laughing with her, being inside her.

Damn, I loved her. I wasn't sure at first, but almost losing her confirmed it for me. I loved Bridgette Turner. If love at first sight was a real thing, that must've been what I felt for her. It didn't make sense, defied logic to feel this way a little over a month into this undeclared relationship, but it was just as tangible for me as the bed we were lying in.

My eyes roved the curves of her body as she lay next to me on her stomach, her head resting on her long arms, her face turned away from me. She was naked and uncovered, a huge intricate flower tattoo with lines I'd memorized on display at her lower back, just above her perfect ass. She was so beautiful to me, the most beautiful woman I'd ever seen.

Tracing the bright pink flower with my fingertip, I asked the back of her head, "Bridge, you up?"

"Mm-hmm," she hummed and nodded. "You tryna go for round four? I don't think I have the energy, baby."

"Nah, I wanna ask you something."

"Okay."

"When did you get this tattoo?"

"Oh, um…five or six years ago, I think."

"It's beautiful. My fourth favorite part of you."

"I bet I can guess your top three."

I chuckled. "I'm sure you can. What type of flower is this? Your tattoo?"

"A lotus."

"Oh, you like lotuses, huh?"

"They're a lot like me."

"How, other than them being beautiful?"

She rolled over on her side, finally facing me. "They grow in mud. But the flower itself emerges perfect, clean. That's me. I came from some shit, Nole. Drugs, alcohol, a-abuse. I saw...I saw some bad stuff all the time, *every day* until the county took me. I lived in constant fear. Foster care wasn't much better, but the youth home I spent the last few years of my childhood in? It gave me a safe place to sleep and structure and Jo. Then Jo gave me you through South." She scooted up in the bed until she was sitting with her back against the thick, wooden headboard. She looked so delicate, fragile as she continued speaking. "And look at me. I don't have a college degree or anything, but I'm living my dream, making movies. I'm here in your beautiful home every night...with you. I'm a lotus, Nole. I'm clean despite the mud I came from."

My chest tightened at the thought of her being scared, abused, hurt. Yes, I'd lost my dad when I was little and it had hurt like a motherfucker when my mother passed away, but I'd never been scared or abused. I had Ev and a huge extended family. When things were good between me and Neil, I had a twin I'd walk through fire for. My life had been good, and it killed me to know hers hadn't.

My mind filled with thoughts of hunting whoever did this shit to her down and making them meet their expiration date, and at the same time, I wanted to hold her, protect her from her past, make her feel what I held in my heart for her right now. I wanted to do whatever she needed me to do and be whatever she needed me to be. I just wanted to love her. And with all of that inside of me, I looked up at her, and said, "I love you, Bridgette."

She reached down and placed her soft hand on my cheek, letting her thumb caress my top lip. "I love you, too."

Bridgette

"Damn, that's a bad dress!" Jo squealed, as I stepped out of the dressing room and twirled around.

I looked down at myself, then turned and inspected myself in the mirror on the wall in the plush dressing area of Lux. It was one of those high-end boutiques, the type that had chandeliers, served champagne to their customers, and sold dresses the price of a modest year's salary. The dress that currently adorned my body was white and form-fitting with a flowing tail.

"It *is* belligerent, isn't it? It's just rude for a dress to fit like this," I said. "Shit, this dress is out of order *and* in contempt of court!"

"Girl! You are gonna tear the red carpet up in that!"

"You ain't never lied!"

"I'm so excited for you, Bridge! Everett showed me the rough cuts from the movie that Nolan emailed him, and girl, you stole every scene you were in! You were phenomenal!"

"Wasn't I?"

Jo rolled her eyes. "Anyway, are you excited about the premiere? I think it's so cool that it's premiering at the Westland Film Festival! That's huge, Bridge!"

"Yeah, my man stays with the connects, honey. Nolan knows everybody, and they all owe his ass a favor. Man, that turns me on."

"I'm glad y'all worked things out. I know how stubborn your ass can be."

"I'm not stubborn. I just don't take mess. You know that. Anyway, we're good. As long as he's good to me, I'll be good to him. Shoot, I'm thinking about giving my apartment up. Haven't been back there for anything other than to get more clothes to take to Nolan's in a while now."

"Well, I love you two together. You're perfect for each other, just like I knew you would be once I found out he liked you."

"Yeah." I glanced at the clock on the wall. "Oh, I better pay for this and get going. I'm making dinner tonight."

"You're cooking? For real?"

"Anything for my Nole."

"Dang, I'm happy for you, but I was enjoying this. I love my girls, but a sister be needing a break sometimes."

"Is that why you were acting like a freed prisoner at the wrap party, hunching on South on the dancefloor?"

"Yep. Oh well, I'll see if Ms. Sherry wants to hang around and chat for a while before she leaves. I can get the dress for you if you want. It can be a bonus. You deserve one."

"Oh, I got it. Nolan gave me his credit card."

"Dayum! His credit card? Girl, what you got between your legs? A saber-toothed tiger?"

"Like you can talk."

I ducked back in the dressing room and took the dress off, I had redressed in my clothes and was about to leave the dressing room when I got a text from Nolan.

Roots: *Hey, you find a dress?*

Me: *Yep, and I look gooood in it.*

Roots: *I bet you do. Can't wait to see you in it. Just wanted to let you know I'll be a little late getting home tonight. Still in editing hell.*

Me: *Don't be too late. Remember, I'm fixing dinner and I'm on the menu for dessert.*

Roots: *You're gonna make me leave now and abandon all my director duties. Love you. See you later.*

Me: *Love you too.*

*****

Nolan

"Baby, I'm home," I said, as I stepped inside my house, placing the mail on the little table next to the front door. It was eight that evening, and I was starving. I couldn't wait to dig into whatever Bridgette had made.

"Go to the dining room!" she called from somewhere. Not the dining room, because when I made it in there, she was nowhere to be found. The table was set, candles were lit, and Smokey Robinson's *Cruisin'* was oozing from the wall-mounted, wireless speakers in the room like thick honey. As I took a seat at the table, I wondered how she managed to find that album among the tons in my vinyl collection, but I was glad she did. Relaxing in my chair, I closed my eyes and smiled, thinking about how blessed I was, how incredible my life was.

"Hey."

At the sound of her voice, I opened my eyes and almost passed the hell out. There she stood, wearing a grin and holding two plates in her hands. The only thing covering her body was these rhinestones circling her nipples—they looked like they were glued to her skin—and some panties that were made out of the same tiny rhinestones. Oh, and a blood-red pair of stilettos.

Goooooot. Damn!

My eyes followed her as she rounded the table. After she set my plate of food in front of me and turned to leave, I saw that they were thong panties and my dick tried its best to bust through my pants.

She took the seat opposite mine and smiled at me. "Dig in. I drove all the way across town to get these steak dinners, then had to take them out of the containers and put them on these plates. I'm exhausted."

I couldn't take my eyes off her as I licked my lips and adjusted in my chair. "Yeah, that sounds like hard work, baby. Uh, what's that you got on?"

Looking down at herself, she said, "This? Just a little something I picked up. You like?" She stood and spun around.

"Uh-huh. Come here, baby."

She did as I requested, stopping next to my chair. "Yes, Nolan?"

I pushed my plate out of the way, stood from my seat, and grabbed her at the hips, lifting her onto the table.

As I flicked my tongue over those titty rhinestones, she said, "But you didn't eat. The steak is medium well, just how you like it, and look at the marbling. Don't you wanna eat first?"

"Nope."

Seconds later, I was inside her with my eyes rolling to the back of my head, my hands clutching her thighs, and my mouth dragging down her long legs that were up in the air while Smokey crooned in the background. At first, I took it slow, giving her controlled strokes, but when it got too good for me to keep my composure, I started pounding into her like a mad man, out of rhythm with the music as her moans and whimpers drove me wild. It didn't help that hers was the best pussy I'd ever had, hands down.

As the seconds wore into minutes, sweat dripped from my skin onto hers, my legs ached, my heart was into a full sprint, and my back stung from the nails Bridgette had dug into my skin, but I loved all of it. *Needed* all of it.

Leaning in, I kissed her while stroking her clit with my fingers, knowing I was about to come and wanting to take her with me. I watched her throw her head back, eyes wide, mouth in an "O" as she pulsated around my dick, and the sight of her losing control in the midst of her orgasm sent me over the edge. Bracing myself, I covered her breasts with my hands, tossed my head back, and roared as I emptied inside her.

20

Bridgette

I felt like a star, like the red carpet was rolled out just for me and this was the premiere of a *Bridgette Turner* movie and all these people had run out and bought expensive clothes because, by chance, *I* might notice them. I was floating in my Balenciaga slash heel pumps, inches taller than Nolan in a white tuxedo that made my entire pelvic region throb. We smiled and posed for the cameras, his hand on the small of my back. This was his night, the debut of his dream, his vision, but it felt like it was my night, too, and maybe that was because of our connection, a bond that didn't make sense, but did. A love that developed too quickly for it to be real but was palpable in its factuality.

Jo and Everett were there, as well as Leland and Kim, Kat, Neil, Honey and her entourage, Nyles and Trevia, and other cast and crew members. Big name stars like got-damn Chadwick Boseman were in attendance, too. Yeah, *Chadwick Boseman*. It seemed half of Hollywood was in Palm Springs for the festival and for the premiere of my movie. The air was electric, and I knew in my soul that after this night, my life would never be the same.

And after I took my seat in that theater and saw the finished product for the first time with the score added and the edits completed? I understood the full genius of the man sitting beside me. Nolan directed the shit out of that movie, and he didn't even take the budgeted director's fee. He was amazing, and he was all mine.

All mine.

Nolan

They loved it. I knew they would, was confident in what we'd created, but still, hearing the applause? It was like nothing I'd ever experienced. It was fucking soul-stirring. I mean, I knew filmmaking was my thing, but to actually live in the midst of a dream was just…surreal. Surreal and unreal.

Our after-party was at a club a friend of mine owned in Palm Springs where I got drunk off my ass, sat next to Bridgette, and damn near screwed her right there at our table. Yeah, it was a good night.

The best night of my life.

21

Nolan

"Who made this potato salad? Got damn, it's good!" Uncle Lee Chester boomed with his mouth full.

It was good, on caliber with Aunt Ever's, but since this was her wedding reception, I knew someone else must've made it. Yeah, after damn near thirty years of shacking up, Aunt Ever and Uncle Lindell tied the knot in the church she'd been baptized in as a little girl. It was a nice wedding, but it was a damn shame Uncle Lindell's first wife had to die for him to finally make things official with Aunt Ever. Nevertheless, I was happy for them.

"Cousin Barbie made it using Aunt Ever's recipe," my sister, Kat, informed him, while bouncing little Leland in her lap. I swear she thought that was her little boy.

"Shit, I think Barbie made hers better than Ever does! Ooowee!" Uncle Lee Chester announced.

"Okay, we can't take it that far," Leland said. "But it's good, though."

"Aw, boy…you just saying that because you Ever's baby. You know Barbie made the shit outta this potato salad," Uncle Lee argued.

"And you grilled the shit outta these ribs. When you gonna tell me your secret?" Bridgette asked, as she licked barbecue sauce from her fingers.

I had to blink and swallow and try not to replace her fingers with my dick in my mind. I was entirely too damn sprung, but shit, what could I do about it?

"Yeah, fire as always, Uncle Lee Chester," Leland's wife, Kim, agreed.

"Thank you, Kimmy," my uncle said, giving her a wink.

Leland shook his head. "Man…"

Kim giggled and kissed Leland on the cheek.

"Bridgette," Uncle Lee continued, "I'll tell you my special dry rub recipe when you tell me how you got Nolan back over on this side of the fence."

"Pardon?" Bridgette asked, confused.

"You know this boy used to didn't never mess with nothing that didn't have straight hair on they vaginises. Now he with you."

Vaginises?

Bridgette pursed her lips, and said, "Uncle Lee, you nasty."

Uncle Lee fell out laughing and wheezing, slapped his knee, coughed, then said, "I always did like you! You tell it like it is!"

"You know it! That's what your nephew likes about me."

"That ain't all I like," I said, kissing her on the cheek.

"Aw, shit! I know that's right, Nephew!" Uncle Lee shouted.

"Wait a damn minute! Where y'all find some banana pudding?!" Bridgette yelled, as Everett and Jo returned to the table.

"On the dessert table," Jo said, reclaiming her seat. "Where you think we found it?"

"I'll be right back, baby. Want me to bring you some?" Bridgette asked, turning to me.

"Yeah. Thanks," I replied.

When Bridgette was out of earshot, Uncle Lee said, "You know what you doing with that, Nephew?" But before I could answer him, he broadcasted, "Got a call!" and tapped that button on his ancient Bluetooth. "What-up-there-now?! Uh-huh…uh-huh? Well, just turn the damn TV off and back on. Shit! This ain't no emergency! Huh? Got-damn, Lou! You can watch *Bonanza* later! Always on my damn nerves about something!"

Everybody at the table was trying to keep from laughing, especially Kim. Uncle Lee was a damn fool, and as much as he and Aunt Lou fought, it was a miracle they'd been together so long.

"Where was I? Oh, yeah! Let me tell you a secret about pleasing black womens, Nolan," he said, his eyes on me, his bushy eyebrows raised.

"Uh, Unc…I know—"

"You gotta stand up when you screw 'em."

Kim spit out her soda and Jo started coughing, choking on her banana pudding. While Everett smacked her on the back, he muttered, "I'm glad we sent the girls to the house with Ms. Sherry."

"Ev, baby, stop helping me. I think you severed my spine!" Jo shrieked.

"My bad, baby."

"See, I know what I'm talking about," Uncle Lee continued. "I ain't fucked laying down since 1984. Now, I know you used to them white girls. They like to be on top. But black women like for you to get that thang from the back. You gotta stand up in it, like that song says. Matter of fact, you need to play that song while you stand up in it. You gotta strip down to your damn church socks and grabbed them hips and pow! Pow! Pow! Gotta hit that jeep spot, Nephew!"

Jeep spot? Did he mean g-spot?

"Unc, I—"

In the midst of me trying to explain that I knew exactly what I was doing with Bridgette, my cousin, Toot, approached the table, and hollered, "Hey, Neil! You with Jo's friend? Man, that's good you moving on from ole girl. You look real neat, too. Got some new clothes? You making all kinds of changes."

The hell?

I frowned. "I'm Nolan. Neil's at Ev's house right now." Neil had decided to skip the reception. I guess attending the wedding was enough social interaction for him. At that moment, I was wishing I'd done the same thing.

"Aw, my bad, cuz. Damn, I just *knew* you was Neil. So you like black chicks now?"

"I've always liked black women, Toot."

"Oh, okay…" He stood there for a minute, staring at me like I was a damn circus freak, then left.

"And another thing…you can't be pulling no black woman's hair. I know Mary Ann and 'nem probably like that shit, but don't try that on no black woman," Uncle Lee said, still trying to give me a damn tutorial. "And my buddy Earl told me he heard some young cats at the barber shop the other day talking about throwing it back in a circle. Now, that must be some of that new-fangled sex stuff that I don't know nothing about, but you might wanna try it—aw, shit. Who is this?" He tapped the Bluetooth button again. "What-up-there-now?! What? Got-damn! The hell you do that for? Shit, I'm on my way!"

Just as Bridgette finally made it back with two plates full of banana pudding, breathlessly informing me that there was a line at the dessert table, Uncle Lee stood, shaking his head, and said, "Gotta go. Lou done knocked my damn nineteen-inch TV down trying to turn it off, talking 'bout she thought she was supposed to unplug it, too. I'll see y'all young folk later. Bye, Kimmy."

"Bye, Uncle Lee," the whole table chorused as he left us, except for Leland, who muttered, "I know the fuck he didn't," while Kim laughed.

"What'd I miss?" Bridgette asked, as she settled in her seat. "I know Uncle Lee been cutting up. He's my favorite part of any Houston trip."

Kim was in tears from laughing. Everett's and Leland's asses were both cackling, too. Jo was giggling, but managed to say, "You missed Uncle Lee giving Nolan instructions on how to handle you in bed."

"Yeah, it was disturbing as hell. He showed his ass in this community center," Kat said.

"Wow, well did you tell him you be handling the shit out of me, baby?" Bridgette asked.

"Didn't get a chance to," I replied.

"Hey, y'all! Looking good, Neil! Nice clothes!" Cousin Barbie said, as she passed our table.

"When did your family start confusing you and Neil?" Bridgette asked, sounding just as perplexed as I felt.

I shook my head and sighed. "Shit, today."

I was wide awake in our room in Aunt Ever's house, my eyes on the ceiling as I thought about Aunt Ever and Uncle Lindell. They were honeymooning in Vegas, thanks to Leland. Both of them were in their seventies, but they looked like teenagers when they left in that limo. They'd waited forever, but they did it. They got married. I honestly never thought about getting married until now. Until Bridgette. Now, I could see myself standing in front of my family saying, "I do." Funny how your idea of happiness can change.

"Nole, you up?" Bridgette asked softly.

I rolled over on my side to see her pretty eyes on me. "Yeah. What you doing up? I thought you were tired."

"I am. I was just wondering…you think this distribution deal with Paramount is gonna happen?"

"Hmm, I think so, if the numbers are right."

"That's huge, Nole. To get a distribution deal like that for your first film? Huge!"

"Yeah, it's gonna be huge for everyone, especially you. You saw how people reacted to your performance at the premiere. The critics are still buzzing about it, and with wide distribution, it can only get better for you."

"I believe that. My agent is already getting all kinds of offers for me to read for parts. For the first time in my career, I'm actually having to pick and choose what I want to pursue. It's crazy!"

"No, it's well-deserved, baby. You put in the work. You earned this."

"So did you. You're the best director I've ever worked with, and I'm not just saying that because I love you."

"Thank you, baby."

After a beat or two of silence, Bridgette sighed. "I always love coming here, to y'all's hometown. I usually stay at South's, but this is nice. Aunt Ever's house is so cozy."

"Yeah, my mom loved this place. She'd be happy to know Aunt Ever is taking good care of it."

"You miss her? Your mom?"

"Every day. My dad, too."

"I wish I knew what that felt like. I wish I could *make* myself miss my family, but I can't."

"I'm sorry it's like that for you, baby."

"You really love me, Nole?"

I raised up in the bed and turned the bedside lamp on, giving her a crazy look. "You know I do, Bridge, with all my heart. You don't believe me?"

I watched as she lay there on her back now, her eyes on the ceiling. Then she turned and glued them to mine. "I do, it's just that there's stuff about me...my name, my *real* name, is Jessie Mae Turner. I changed it when I turned eighteen because I was named after my grandmother and I...I hate her."

No wonder she used to spaz out on me when I mentioned my assistant manager's name—*Jesse*. "She hurt you?" I asked.

Bridgette nodded. "My mother, her daughter, lived with her, was living there when she had me. I grew up there until I was taken from them." She faced the ceiling again. "My grandmother was so mean. She sold drugs, she did drugs, she drank like a fish, and she cursed me out for merely existing. There were always dope fiends hanging around the house...and men. My grandmother loved men. Didn't matter to her if they were married, single, doped up, whatever. Didn't even matter to her if they were her daughter's boyfriends or my father."

"W-what?"

"Yeah, she took my daddy from my mom, was with him until he got locked up for stealing, because he, like my mom, was a crackhead, and it didn't matter that she was sleeping with him. Nobody got a free ride from my grandmother; he had to pay for his fix just like everybody else. I liked my father, because he was the only person who took up for me. He might've been sleeping with my grandmother, but he would curse her out over me. That's more than I can say for my mother. She just let her hurt me. She let it all happen...*everything*."

She reached over on the night table and grabbed her phone, tapped on the screen a few times, and handed it to me. I took it and found an obituary on the screen. An obituary for a Jessie Mae Parker.

"This is your grandmother?" I asked, staring at the old, black and white picture of a beautiful woman. She looked like she could've been a movie star back in the day.

"Yeah. She died a few months back, and I...I was glad when I found out. That's fucked up, isn't it?"

Shaking my head, I said, "Not if she hurt you. She didn't give you any reason to be sad about her passing."

"Her death, or my guilt for being relieved about it, is the reason I accepted Laz's offer to go out. I was in a messed-up head space that night and I just needed to go somewhere and do something, but I wasn't going to sleep with him. I'm not the least bit attracted to that man."

"I didn't think you were, baby. I knew something was up with you. I could tell you were dealing with something."

"Yeah, and I almost got in some mess I never want to be in, but you rescued me, and I'll forever be thankful for that."

I fell onto my back. "I ain't no hero, baby. I knew what Laz had been doing and chose to look the other way like I did everything in that club, because I was always looking out for me, looking for an angle, for some dirt to use to advance my bottom line. I was wrong. That way of living is wrong, and I see that now. If I'd stopped Laz from using *Second Avenue* to do his shit, maybe he would've never gotten to you, never drugged you. You were right; I definitely ain't shit."

"Well, I'm in the same category as you. I didn't call the police on him, because I was worried about *my* bottom line—my career. I can't judge you, and you need to stop being so hard on yourself.

You're a good man, Nole. Flawed, but good, and you get bonus points for loving me."

I reached for her, pulled her to me, and kissed her forehead. "I love the hell out of you, Bridgette Turner."

"I love you, too. Nole?"

"Yeah?"

"There's something I've been wondering about."

"Okay…"

"What's with you and Neil?"

"Uh…what do you mean?"

"Well, you McClains are close. That's one thing I've always loved about y'all. Being Jo's assistant and best friend, I've gotten to spend a lot of time with y'all. You know that."

"Yeah, that's how I came to realize just how remarkable you are."

"Thanks, baby, but what I'm saying is, I don't understand why you and your twin are so distant. I've been basically living with you for months now, and he has never come over for a visit other than that one time before we got together when he came with South. You barely even look at each other at family gatherings. You never bring him up. I've never seen you call him or anything, and when you're in the same room together, you're at each other's throats. Not like the roasting that goes on between you and South and Leland. You two are cut-throat. What's up with that? I mean, I thought twins were supposed to have a special bond or something."

I sighed. "It's…we do have a special bond, or at least we used to."

"What happened?"

I squeezed my eyes shut and told myself that I should've expected this. It was strange. I could admit that, but I hated talking about Neil. Hell, I hated even thinking about him. Nevertheless, I loved this woman, and I owed her my truth. "Uh, Neil is just…he hasn't been right since he and his girlfriend broke up. They'd been together since junior high, basically. It was an on and off thing at first, but they went to the same college and things got serious then. They lived together for years. She even moved out to LA with him, and then, something happened and they broke up."

"What do you mean, 'something happened?' What happened?"

"That's just it. I don't know. He won't talk about it, and neither will she."

"You're still in contact with her?"

"No, but a few years back, she called me at the club to see if I could convince Neil to stop contacting her. They'd been broken up for over a year, and he was still trying to get her back. Evidently, she wasn't interested."

"Wow, how long ago was the break-up?"

"Shit, years. Probably close to seven or eight years now."

"And he's still messed up over her? That's why he's the way he is?"

"Yeah. But anyway, up until the break-up, we were cool. Not as close as we were growing up, because like I told you before, we had become more individual. Had our own sets of friends, our own relationships, but there was no hostility between us. Things weren't like they are now."

"Well, what happened?"

"I'm getting to that baby. I mean, it's not black and white. It's not something he or I did. It's just...because of our connection, I feel what he feels, and after his and Emery's break-up, the only thing I felt from Neil was depression and darkness and guilt, and because he wouldn't tell me what happened, it was confusing as hell, and shit, who wants to feel like that all the time? So, more and more, I distanced myself from him. Barely called him, and it just progressed to where it is now."

"You two act like you hate each other with the way you argue every time you're in the same room."

"In a way, I do hate him, or at least his weakness and his inability to move the fuck on with his life. He's a drunk and a gambler and no telling what else and it doesn't make any sense. Neil is a damn genius. He can play several instruments and compose music, can take the most compelling photographs, can write poetry, can even paint. We had plans, you know? I was gonna make movies and he would score them. Shit, he should be the most successful of all of us, but instead, he chooses to waste the hell away over a woman who has moved on with her life. She's married!"

A minute passed before she said, "Did you…have you ever tried to help him, Nole?" She was delicate in her approach, but the question still hit a nerve.

"Of course I have. We all have—Ev, Leland, Kat. He doesn't want it. That's why Ev is basically running his life now. None of us want to see him like this."

She didn't give me a response.

"You think I haven't tried hard enough, don't you? You think I should do more to help him because he's my twin?"

"Do you think you should do more to help him because he's your twin?"

"I…I don't know, Bridge."

"I think—never mind."

"No, tell me."

She moved from her spot on the bed and climbed on top of me, straddling me. "I think you should at least try to mend things with him. He's your brother. I hate that you two fight all the time."

"I don't know how to do that. I don't even know if he'd want to do that."

"You can try, and if he rejects you, it's on him."

I thought about that for a minute and had to admit it made sense. So I said, "Okay. I'll try."

22

Bridgette

Eight million dollars.

That was how much Paramount paid for the distribution rights to *Floetic Lustice*. Eight million dollars for a small film, written by an unknown screenwriter and shot over a span of two months with limited sets, a small crew, and a first-time director.

Eight.

Million.

Dollars.

And they were expediting the wide release. This would be the first film I'd acted in that would actually be seen by more than a few people in two or three theaters in LA and New York, just so it would be eligible for awards season and then sent straight to the DVD market. Nolan's movie would be seen across the country on many screens, and news of the distribution deal had spread so wildly that anyone connected with the movie was now a hot commodity for the entertainment blogs, internet shows, and morning talk shows. I had been invited to the *Loretha Halter Show*. I'd always admired how she parlayed a popular Instagram account into a Wendy Williams-esque TV show. She could be shady, much like Wendy, but Loretha always came off more genuine and real, in my opinion.

Sitting in Nolan's living room, playing with little Nat—because I'd been missing my godbaby and decided to rescue her from that bougie daycare and spend this Friday with her—I was almost overwhelmed with gratitude. My career was taking off, I had great friends, and my man? He was more than I even had sense enough to hope for. He wasn't perfect, but he was mine, and I believed in my heart that he was made for me.

Speaking of my man, I looked up to see him sitting on the sofa with his laptop balanced on his thighs, but his eyes were on me and Nat. He'd decided to stay home with me today but was supposed to be handling some McClain Films work.

"Aren't you supposed to be working instead of grinning at me and Nat?" I asked.

"You're good with her. I like watching y'all."

I reached over and rubbed my hand through the bush of curly hair on Nat's head. "Me and Nat are BFFs. Didn't you know?"

"Yeah. You want kids, Bridge?" Nolan asked, catching me a little off-guard. I was hoping this subject wouldn't come up for a while longer. My answer tended to shift things in my relationships.

"Um, to be honest...no. I know that's weird, because who doesn't want kids, right? But I just don't. My career is kind of like my baby, you know? I'm focused on taking care of it. Plus, I got two godbabies. I just wanna be a good Teetee Bridgette to them. I always wanted to be someone's favorite auntie, but I'm an only child, so I didn't think it could happen." I ended my statement and waited for him to tell me to get my stuff and leave because he came from a big family and wanted ten sons.

"I feel you. I like being an uncle, too. You get the kids without the diaper changes and stuff."

"So...you're okay with me not wanting kids. I mean, it's not like you're gonna marry me or anything like that, but I'm just saying...if we were to have a future together, you wouldn't want kids?"

"Bridgette, in case you haven't noticed, I'm focused on my career, too. McClain Films is in its infancy, and all I can think about, all I care about besides you, is growing it. I wanna build this company into an empire and travel the globe. I wouldn't want to bring any children into the world knowing I'm so committed to my work. And if *I'm* being honest, I'd have to admit that I never really wanted kids, either."

I squinted at him. "Are you serious, or are you just saying that?"

"I'm serious, baby. I'm a lot of things, but I'm not a liar."

I tucked my lips between my teeth and glanced at Nat, who was staring at Peppa Pig on the TV screen. Then I shifted my eyes back to Nolan. "If Nat wasn't here right now, I would show you how much what you just said turns me on."

He raised an eyebrow and licked his lips. "Uh...ain't it about time for Jo to pick her up? No rush, but..." He lowered his voice to a whisper. "Damnnnn, I want you right now."

I turned to Nat to see her staring at me, and to play it off, asked, "Is that a new lion you got there, Nat? It's so cool!" like it was my first time noticing the thing. That child had to own at least a thousand stuffed lions.

"Yep! My daddy gave it to me!"

"Really?" Dang, when did she start calling Stupid-Ass-Sid "daddy?" This was a new development.

"Yeah! I love it! He got my sister one, too!"

Sid bought Lena a toy and South let him? What was going on over in Calabasas? "Nat, what's your daddy's name?" I asked.

"Ebbwitt!" she said, as if I should've already known the answer. Nolan and I exchanged a surprised look, but to be honest, it made my heart melt. Before I could comment, my phone began to buzz.

"Hey, girl! You on your way?" I said, after seeing that it was Jo calling.

"Yeah, but have you talked to Sage?"

"Actually, no. I've been trying to reach her for over a week to see if she'll be available to do my makeup for the *Loretha Halter Show*. I don't like the way her people do hers."

"Me either. They have her casket-ready every week!"

"Right! So you haven't been able to reach her, either?"

"No. I was trying to see if she could hook me up for this ridiculous post-baby photo shoot Ev wants me to do. He's even picked the outfits out, and all of them are showing way too much boob. He is so obsessed with my boobs now that I'm breastfeeding."

"Well, they *are* gargantuan…"

"Whatever. I think I'ma drop by her place tomorrow."

"Okay, keep me posted. I know she said life was getting her down. I hope nothing serious is going on."

"Me, too. Anyway, I'll be there in about twenty minutes."

"I got a fine man over here making eyes at me, so speed it up."

"Ew, let me come get my baby out of that den of iniquity."

"You better, because we finna be iniquitying all over this house."

"Nasty ass."

"I love you, too."

Nolan

I walked into the master suite bathroom in my house and scanned the boxes crowding the floor. It was a huge bathroom with a dual-sink vanity, toilet, garden tub, and a neo-angle shower with a built-in bench. This bathroom was what made me buy the house when I decided to sell the one Everett bought me and upgrade, but my lady's possessions were making the space look like a coat closet.

"It's a lot, I know. Having second thoughts about me moving in?" I hadn't noticed she'd stopped organizing her makeup on the counter and was looking at me.

"Bridge, you moved in months ago, right after Montana. Did you forget about that?"

"You know what I mean. Before, if anything went wrong, you could kick me out knowing I had an apartment to go back to. Now that I've given my apartment up and made this my official address, seems like things are—I don't know—heavy, serious."

"So, you weren't serious about us before now?"

"You know I was. I'm just…I know this is a lot of shit, okay? You probably want me to get rid of some of it. Hell, I *need* to get rid of some of it..."

"Naw, it's fine, baby. If you need it, keep it. Shit, if you want it, keep it. Whatever makes you happy."

"Thanks, Nole," she said, stepping over a box to give me a kiss.

While she organized what looked like a thousand tubes of lipstick, I tilted my head to the side, inspecting the contents of a box sitting on the floor. "I didn't know you collected eggs."

"I don't," she said, without turning around.

I picked up a green one. It was cool to the touch, made of some kind of stone. "Well, you got like ten of them in this box, different sizes, too."

She finally turned to look at me. "Oh, those! Those are yoni eggs. I don't collect them. I use them. I need to find a special place for those in here."

"Use them for what?"

"To strengthen the muscles in my...yoni."

I frowned, setting the green one down and picking up the pink one. "How?"

"By putting it inside me."

"You put these...this some kind of little dildo or something?"

"No, you see that long, wand-shaped stone? It's called a yoni wand and it's a sort of dildo or can be used as one, at least. I just told you the eggs are used to strengthen the yoni muscles and they have other benefits, too."

"Really? Like what?"

"Uh..." She reached over and took the pink egg from me. "They help increase lubrication—make that thang real juicy—they heighten sexual desire, make orgasms more intense, help you to be better able to have vaginal orgasms, tighten the vajayjay—"

"Got damn, that explains it! That motherfucker is like a vice grip!"

"Wow, okay."

"No, really! Haven't you noticed I can only go like twenty-five minutes now? That's why!"

"Yeah, I actually did notice that..."

"How often do you use these?" I asked.

"Not that often since we've been together. You won't give my poor vagina a long enough break for me to use them."

"Shit, I can't. Hey, why do they come in different sizes?"

"Um, the goal with the yoni eggs is for you to use your muscles down there to hold the egg in place. The smaller the egg you're able to hold, the stronger the muscles."

"And the tighter the pussy?"

"Well, yeah, you could say that."

"I bet your ass can hold a damn microscopic one."

"I don't know now that you been stretching me the hell out."

I grinned. "So, what do you do with these little rocks? You put them in you, too?"

"No, baby, and they're crystals, not rocks. They're for coochie weight-lifting."

"Um, what?"

She giggled. "Okay, you see this little hole that's been drilled into the end of the egg?"

I nodded.

"I loop a string through it and tie a pouch to the end of the string, then I put the egg inside me, leave the pouch dangling outside of me, and put the crystals in it. I squeeze my muscles down there to hold the egg in place with the added weight of the crystals and then release it. I do some reps for like fifteen minutes and then take it out."

"Shit."

"Yeah, I know it's weird, but it works. It amplifies what the yoni egg does alone."

"No, I *know* it works. I meant shit, that turns me on. Let's fuck."

"How you gonna say, 'let's fuck,' like I'm some THOT off the street?"

"My bad, baby. I just…"

"Take your damn clothes off and lay your ass down so I can be on top and we can be done in time for me to get ready for dinner," she said, leaving the bathroom.

As I followed her to the bed, I said, "Yes, ma'am."

"And don't forget to smack my thighs while I'm riding you."

"When do I ever forget to do that?"

I couldn't believe I'd agreed to doing this. It was guaranteed to be a disaster, but I'd let Bridgette talk me into it, because shit, she could talk me into just about anything.

"It's gonna be okay. You know that, right?" she asked, resting her hand on my knee.

I shifted on the sofa and nodded. "Yeah." Letting my eyes inspect her, I asked, "Why you wearing that?"

She frowned as she looked down at the little black dress she had on. "What's wrong with this?"

"It's short, and you got on heels."

"You like for me to wear short dresses and heels. I'm tryna look nice for you."

"And Neil?"

"No, for *you*, but do you want me to look raggedy in front of your brother? I would think you'd want me to look good."

"Not *that* good. He's just coming over for dinner, not a damn cocktail party."

"You're trippin'. What do you think is gonna happen? You think I'ma trade you in for Neil after what you just put on me?"

"I did put it on you, didn't I?"

"Wow."

I shrugged. "Am I lying?"

"Anyhow, you think I want him because he's your twin or something?"

I tilted my head to the side, taking her in, and then said, "Never mind. You're way outta his league. He couldn't handle you even if I gave his ass instructions."

"Um, thank you, I guess?"

147

"You're welcome. Look, I just don't want him looking at you and shit. This?" I swept my finger up and down the front of her body. "All of this? It's mine."

"Uh, I know that."

"Just making sure."

Rolling her eyes, she asked, "You want me to change, Nole? Would that make you feel better? I'll change before I let you treat your brother like shit because you *think* he's looking at me. I'm serious about wanting things to improve between you two."

I closed my eyes and sighed. "I'm sorry, baby. This whole dinner with Neil thing is fucking with me. Shit, I can't believe he agreed to come when I asked."

"You told him you wanted the two of you to do better with each other, right?"

"Yeah, but still, this is weird. Hell, I was shocked he answered my call at all."

"Well, maybe he wants to reconnect and mend things, too. Maybe all that needed to happen was for you to make the first move."

As she scooted closer to me and leaned against me, I wrapped an arm around her, and said, "Yeah, maybe."

"So, do you like working with South? I love working for Jo," Bridgette said, carrying the conversation with Neil like she had been since we sat down to eat the Indian food she'd had delivered. He hadn't had much to say and neither had I. I guess we were both feeling awkward being in the same space without tearing each other down.

Neil shrugged. "It's a'ight, I guess. Not exactly my dream job, but Ev ain't gonna let me off the hook, so I gotta do what I gotta do."

"Yeah, Ev thinks he's everybody's daddy," I chimed in, finally getting used to Neil being there, and seeing as he was my damn twin, it was pitiful that I had to adjust to his presence. Bridgette was right about the state of our relationship being sad.

"And shit, we go along with it, because he was our daddy for so long," Neil pointed out.

"True, true. Remember that time he tried to spank Leland for breaking a glass while Mama was at work?"

Neil smiled. "Yeah, and Leland's little ass took off running before Ev could even get his hands on a belt. Ev ran after him but ended up tripping over something in the front yard and hurting his ankle. Then he was really mad!"

"But Leland was so damn fast! Ev still couldn't catch him! Leland was Fastlane McClain even back then. What was he? Like four or five?"

"Yeah, I think so."

"Ev kept our asses in line, though. Kept us out of trouble."

"Yeah, he did. Man, those were some good times. Shit was simple back then, you know?"

"It sure was," I agreed. "But life is good now. I ain't got no complaints." I reached across the table and grasped Bridgette's hand as she smiled at me.

"Aye, man...I know I was talking shit at the hospital, but I'm happy for you. I can tell she's good for you," Neil said, and I damn near fainted.

"He's good for me, too," Bridgette said.

"Y'all hold on to that. Ain't nothing like having someone you love who loves you back. That shit is rare. Most of us never get it," Neil shared, his eyes on his plate.

"Man, if I could get and keep her? Your one is out there. Believe that," I said.

Neil shook his head. "I don't know, man."

"She is, Neil. You just gotta be ready for her, be ready to be the man she needs. You know?"

He looked up at me and gave me a slow nod. "Yeah, I see what you're saying."

We finished dinner, had coffee instead of drinks since Neil had that little issue with alcohol, sat in the living room and chopped it up about everything from music to movies, and when he left a little before midnight, we shared a hug. While Bridgette and I stood in the front doorway and watched Neil back out of my driveway, I said, "Thank you for tonight, baby."

She kissed my cheek, and replied, "This was all you, Nole, and I'm so proud of you."

I slid my arm around her waist and squeezed her to me, closing my eyes and thanking God for creating this woman for me.

23

Bridgette

I had been interviewed so many times, I was just about interviewed out. The *Floetic Lustice* press junket was jam-packed, hectic, and demanding. I was tired, *exhausted*, but I wouldn't have gotten off that ride if someone paid me a million dollars to. I loved every minute of being in makeup chairs and greenrooms. I loved doing cast interviews and solo interviews. I loved being on morning shows and web shows and radio shows. I loved the compliments about my performance and the offers that were pouring in for more movie roles, *starring* movie roles. But most of all, I loved that Nolan was there with me every step of the way. As the director, he was a part of some interviews, and the ones he wasn't a part of, he still accompanied me to, hanging out in the greenroom or dressing room until I was done.

Everything was falling into place in my life—my career was taking off so fast, I could barely keep up with it. For the first time in my life, I could see myself becoming someone's wife, because if Nolan popped the question, I was going to scream YES! It didn't matter to me that we'd only been together a few months. He loved me, and I loved him. I'd never known what that felt like until Nolan.

Until now.

And I never wanted to lose that feeling. I never wanted to lose *him*.

*****

My foot wouldn't stop tapping in my Gucci pumps as I sat on the couch in the greenroom, staring at the selfie I'd posted on IG minutes earlier. Cocking my head to the side, I asked, "You think I need to get a boob job?"

My eyes shifted to Nolan sitting beside me, who looked up from his own phone, and said, "What?"

"A boob job. You think I need one?"

"What, like implants?"

I nodded.

"Naw, baby. You're perfect."

Grinning, I leaned in and kissed his cheek. "I'm glad you think so, but I think it would help me fill out my clothes better. I'm a solid C-cup, but I think my frame could handle some Ds."

Setting his phone down, he fixed his eyes on me. "Where is this coming from? I've never known you to be self-conscious about your body. You've gotta be the most confident woman I've ever known."

"I have issues with my booty, too."

"Now I know something's wrong, because I have never seen anything as remarkable as your ass."

Now he really had me cheesing. "Really, Nole?"

"Hell, yeah! What's going on, baby? What's wrong? You nervous about this interview?"

I sighed and lowered my eyes to my lap. "Yeah, I am."

"Why? You've been on some big-time shows already. This show doesn't even have as big an audience as some of the web shows you've been on."

"Yeah, but this show's audience is known for roasting the guests. Have you ever read the comments on the *Loretha Halter Show* IG page, or the ones under the show snippets they post on YouTube? They're brutal!"

"Then don't read the damn comments. Shit, fuck those trolls. I know you're not going to let them make you miss out on an opportunity to get your shine on."

"Plus this show is known for showing horrible old pictures of the guests. I don't know if I can take the embarrassment," I continued, not responding to his encouragement.

"Baby, look at me," he said.

I did.

"You're Bridgette-Motherfucking-Turner. You got this."

Reaching up and resting my hand on his cheek, I smiled. "I love you, you know that?"

"I love you, too."

"I wish you were going out there with me."

"I can. Want me to talk to the producers?"

I shook my head. "I'm on in a few minutes. I'll be okay."

"I know you will."

Fifteen minutes later, I was sitting on Loretha's orange couch, legs crossed, looking fierce in a mixed-print, floral and black, cold-shoulder Louis Vuitton dress and those Gucci heels, my shoulder-length hair up in a bun, and a ridiculous beat on my face courtesy of Sage. Yeah, I was finally able to track her down. Loretha was funny and friendly—as I knew she'd be—and I quickly relaxed in front of her and her studio audience as I fielded her questions about the movie, working with Honey Combs, and how fine Nyles Adams was in person.

Then she turned to her audience, and said, "You know how we love surprises on this show, right?"

The audience cheered and hooted in response.

"What y'all know?" she responded, uttering her signature catchphrase with the crowd quickly answering her with, "Oh, we know!" as they always did.

"Okay," she continued, "We have a special guest who can't wait to share the couch with Bridgette here. You ready, Bridgette?"

With wide eyes, I shrugged and smiled. "I guess I better be." I turned to watch as Nolan stepped onto the stage looking like four gourmet meals in his tan slacks and dark brown sweater, only it wasn't Nolan being escorted onstage by one of the producers.

It was my mother.

24

Nolan

I leaned forward, my eyes on the monitor in the greenroom. Bridgette was killing this interview, just like she did all the others. She was a natural in front of any camera, and while I had to agree that the *Loretha Halter Show* was a little on the ratchet side, like it was the *Love and Hip Hop* of talk shows, all press was good press as far as I was concerned. And as far as the trolls that loved the show so much? Hell, Bridgette was the most articulate woman I knew. She knew how to put on whatever character she needed to put on to get the job done. She wasn't giving them any fuel to use against her.

My phone buzzed in my hand, and my eyes widened when I looked down to see Neil's name on the screen. "Hello?" I answered, hoping he wasn't into some shit. Then I felt like shit for that being my first reaction to him calling me.

"Hey, Nolan?"

"Yeah, what's going on?"

"Uh, I just wanted to call, and…shit. I don't want nothing, but I was just thinking about how when we were kids, we would stay up late talking and shit, You remember that?"

"Yeah, yeah. We'd talk about everything and nothing at all, kid shit that we thought was important at the time," I said, through a chuckle.

"Man, I miss that, having someone I can talk to about anything. I mean, I know I done kinda burnt my bridges and everything with this bullshit I been on, but still…"

I nodded. "I hear you. Hey, man…if you need to talk, I'm here for you. We still twins, no matter what's gone down."

"For real, Nole?"

"Yeah, and I apologize for being so distant with you."

"And for being an arrogant asshole?"

"Damn, okay…that, too."

"Well, I'm sorry for fucking with you for dating all those colonizers."

"Uh, okay…it's all good. Hey, man—"

Bridgette burst through the greenroom door, and my eyes shot to the monitor where I could see Loretha Halter standing from her ugly-ass yellow chair, talking to the audience, and an older woman sitting on the orange couch, inches from where Bridgette was supposed to be sitting.

I shot to my feet, mumbled, "Neil, I gotta go," into the phone, and ended the call. "Bridge, what's going on?"

She was shaking all over, visibly shaking, as her eyes wandered the room, not focusing on anything. She didn't respond to my question, and I wondered if she'd heard me.

"Bridge?" I said softly. "What's wrong?"

A knock came at the door, and one of the producers, a petite brunette woman, peeked her head in, headset still in place. Before she could speak, I shifted my attention from Bridgette to her and asked, "What's going on? What happened?"

"They ambushed me, that's what happened. They invited my-my-my mother on the show! My fucking mother is out there, and no one told me she'd be here! That's what happened!" Bridgette shrieked. The shaking had grown worse, her eyes wilder. I knew if I didn't get her out of there, she was going to have a full melt-down, and I was afraid of just what that might look like.

So I grasped her arm and moved in close to her ear. "Let me take you home, baby."

Her eyes shot up to my face and she frowned. "W-what?"

"Let's go home. Let me take you home. Okay?"

I could see the tears filling her eyes and my heart fell to my damn feet. I had never, not once in the six or so months we'd been together, seen her shed a tear. She'd once told me she stopped crying when she was a kid. But at that moment, she was on the edge of crying.

"Nolan...my mother is out there."

I nodded. "I know. Let's go home, okay? We'll go home and we can talk about it if you want."

"We need to mic her again and get her back on the couch," the producer decided to announce as if, for even a second, I gave a fuck about that show.

"That's not happening," I said, wrapping my arm around Bridgette's waist and leading her out of the room.

"But we were promised a full interview," she tried.

"And you chose to ambush her with an estranged family member. You'll be lucky if she doesn't sue."

"Sue for what?!"

I shrugged. "We'll think of something."

She said something else, but I ignored it.

A few minutes later, I helped Bridgette into my car, buckled her in, and took her home.

I didn't cry.

The tears came, but I didn't let even one fall. I fought them as hard as I could, and I won.

I don't cry. I never cry.

I feel pain, experience sorrow, my heart aches, but I do not cry.

Not since that day when I was eleven years old, crouched in my grandmother's closet, praying and crying and begging for a way out. Not since she called me a weak-ass cry-baby. Not one tear had fallen from my eyes. Not. One. Because I wasn't nobody's damn cry-baby.

I didn't cry when Nolan buckled my seatbelt like I was a kid, because my trembling hands wouldn't let me do it myself. I didn't cry when he carried me into the house, sat me on our bed, and undressed me. My eyes were dry when he carried me to the shower, sat me on the bench inside of it, and washed me. I might've been shaking like a leaf, but I didn't weep when he begged me to eat and finally just fed me. And now, lying in his arms, I still refused to shed a tear.

But I needed to. I knew I'd feel better if I did. I just…couldn't. If I did, she'd win. Even in her grave, she'd win.

And I couldn't let her win.

I couldn't let myself experience that relief, because if I did, I knew I'd hear her voice in my head.

"You damn cry-baby! I'ma give your ass something to cry about! Ain't nothing wrong with you!"

I snuggled closer to Nolan, tried to fuse my skin with his. I wished I could crawl inside him, be coated in him, lose myself in him. He was my refuge. He was my safety net, and although I knew he was giving me his all, I still selfishly wished he had more to give, because I was a glutton for him.

"Can't sleep?" His rich voice vibrated in his chest.

"No. Did I wake you?"

"No. I can't sleep, either."

I adjusted my head on his hard chest. "I'm sorry I messed up, running off that set like that. I know that looked bad for the film, your company…"

"Do you really think I care about any of that right now? The only thing I'm concerned about is you, baby."

"Folks are probably dragging me all over social media right now. Where's my phone?"

"Turned off and in your purse."

"I need to see it."

"No, you don't."

"I have to at least call Jo," I tried.

"I already texted her and told her I got you. And I do got you. You know that, right? That I got you no matter what?"

"Yeah…"

"And you know you can tell me anything? Anything, baby, and it won't change how I feel about you."

"I know."

"So…you wanna talk about why what happened, happened?"

"There's nothing to talk about. I saw her walk out there, and I just lost it. I…I never thought I'd see her again. Never *wanted* to see her again, but there she was. Looking like…shit, she looked like life had wrung her out and thrown her away. And it just felt like a damn conspiracy or something. The devilish look in Loretha's eyes? I knew she could be messy, but…I wonder how she even got in contact with her?"

"I'ma find out, and when I get through with her ass, she's gonna be in the unemployment line, just like Mike and Rourke."

I sat straight up and yelled, "What?! Did you…how?"

"Like I said, people owe me favors, and when I need to cash them in, I cash them in."

"You got them fired? What if they want revenge or something? Losing a job is a big thing."

"They won't mess with us. They know I can do worse, and I will if they push me. Anyway, they got new jobs. I made sure of that."

"You got that kinda pull? For real?"

"I got those kinda connects. I told you that."

"Damn…but why get them fired and then hired by someone else?"

"To show them I could, so they'd think twice about fucking with you again. Look, they knew better than that shit they pulled. They knew me well enough to know I wasn't playing with you. They knew this wasn't what I had with anyone else. I almost lost you over that shit, so they had to be penalized."

"Damn, Nole."

"Like I said before, I ain't no saint."

"I know..."

I don't know what it was about Nolan having power, or me hearing or seeing evidence of that power even if it was just in his tone of voice, but it turned me all the way on and I found myself climbing on top of him in the dark bedroom. I kissed him, rubbed my hands up and down his chest, grabbed a nipple and twisted it, slid my hand between us and grabbed his erection through his underwear, scooted down his body, put him in my mouth, and sucked his dick like it was a lollipop all while he asked over and over again what I was doing and if I was sure I felt like doing it.

I didn't answer, because I knew I should've been working through my feelings regarding seeing my mother again and dissecting my reaction to being in her presence which made the years of therapy I underwent look like I sat in Dr. Crawford's office hula-hooping. I should've been crying, even screaming, to purge myself of the hurt and pain that'd been dredged up from her first little surprise phone call. Hell, I needed to apologize to Karen, have tea with Jo, fall on my knees and pray. *Something.* But instead, I sank down on his shaft, grinding against his pelvis, letting him fill me to a point that it was actually uncomfortable, but I needed to feel it. I needed to feel the pleasure and pain and that out-of-control overwhelmingly intense feeling that accompanied a good orgasm. I needed to experience him clutching my ass or my hips to control my ride. I needed the warmth of his breath against my skin, the abrasiveness of his teeth grazing my nipples, the smoothness of his tongue in my mouth, and the mingling of our sweat as the minutes rolled into each other.

And I felt all of that.

And it was divine.

25

Bridgette

I groaned when the ringing of my cell phone woke me up, then remembered Nolan turning it off and banning me from using it. So I figured it was his and not mine.

"Baby, your phone," I muttered, reaching over to touch him and feeling nothing but soft sheets. Popping an eye open, I confirmed that his side of the bed was empty, and a turn of my head showed me my first thought was correct. It *was* my phone. I guessed I was off phone restriction now.

It'd stopped ringing when I picked it up, rubbed my eyes, and checked the screen. Nolan. He'd already left? I checked the time— 9:00 AM. Damn, I'd slept late, exhausted from that *Lord of the Rings Trilogy* sex he put on me. Tapping on his name, I activated the speakerphone and rested my head on the pillow.

He answered my call with, "Did I wake you?"

"Yeah, but I needed to get up anyway. Why didn't you wake me up before you left?"

"I woke up late myself, and since you were laying there naked, I knew waking you up was a bad idea."

"Why you say that?"

"You know why. Shit, I probably wouldn't have made it to the office and I got a lot of stuff to do. Gotta meeting with Ev. Got lawyers to talk to about this script I wanna option. If I'd woken you up? None of that would get done and I need to do this stuff so I can buy you some more of them eggs and crystals."

"I can buy my own."

"I know."

"Anyway, you act like I'm irresistible or something."

"Shit, you are."

"And that's a problem?"

"Yeah, but it ain't a problem I'm tryna solve. Hey, I made some coffee and there's a surprise coming in about an hour, so get up. I'll see you this evening. Love you."

Before I could ask about the surprise, he hung up.

I'd just managed to shower and throw on a romper when the doorbell rang, signaling the arrival of five Russian women who were there to give me a full-on spa treatment right there at the house. I couldn't help but wonder if Nolan had screwed any of them but knew that he knew better. One thing about Nolan, he wasn't messy. As many times as we'd been out together and as long as I'd been living with him, I'd never been approached by any of his exes, if you could call them that. But for all I knew, they lived at *The Gallery.*

Anyway, I can't lie and say I wasn't excited about my spa day, and when I read the card one of the women presented to me, my heart swelled in my chest.

Relax and enjoy being spoiled. You deserve it more than I deserve you. I love you, and when you're ready to talk, I'm here.

Nolan

*****

"Damn, this tea is good. The spa Russians made it?"

Taking my cup from Jo, I nodded. "Yep."

"I'ma have to put a bug in Everett's ear about this. Look at you! Your skin is glowing; your nails are painted all cute. What color is that?"

"Mint."

"I love it! Hell, I need to be spoiled, too."

"Bitch, that man bought you a whole entire jet, you live in a palace, and you have a cook, a maid, and two damn nannies!"

"Correction, one is just a backup nanny."

"Uh-huh. You get driven around by bodyguards, you own at least ten pairs of Loubs, your push present was a damn Bentley. Your ass needs to shut up."

"I still want a home spa day, though," she mumbled.

"Then tell South and watch him have a fully-staffed spa built onto your house with his supercalifragilisticexpiali-extra ass."

"You ain't lying."

"Got that man super sprung."

"Look who's talking!"

We both laughed.

"So, you know I came to check on you. I saw what happened on the *Loretha Halter Show*..." Jo began.

"And you see that I'm fine. I'm good."

"You sure? I know how you feel about—"

"I'm good, Jo. I am. It was just a shock, you know? But I'm back to normal now."

"Okay, so did you talk to Nolan?"

I frowned. "About what?"

"About why you reacted to seeing your mom like you did?"

I leaned back on the sofa, cradling my mug in my hands. "I told him I had a fucked-up childhood awhile back. Shared some of what I went through."

"But not all of it?"

"No."

"You should."

"He doesn't need to know all that. It's not important."

"He loves you, it *is* important, and he should know."

"I meant to ask you, when did Nat start calling South 'Daddy?'"

"You're shutting down on me like you usually do, huh?"

I just looked at her with raised eyebrows. She knew the drill. If I didn't want to talk about something, no one could make me. Not even her.

Through a sigh, she said, "Everett always refers to himself as

'Daddy' when he's talking to Lena, so Nat just started calling him that. I didn't correct her, because hell, he *is* her daddy in all the ways that count."

"Sid's okay with this?"

"He doesn't know. He might never know, because his little visits are few and far between now. Not that I'm complaining."

My phone buzzed, and I didn't realize I was grinning while reading Nolan's *on my way home* text until Jo said, "Damn, a text got you cheesing like that? Must be *Lord of the Rings Trilogy.*"

"Who?"

"*Lord of the Rings Trilogy.* Nolan?"

"Oh, as of today, I'm calling him *War and Peace.*"

"Damn, that book is over a thousand pages long!"

"Exactly."

"You are so damn crazy!" Jo said, doubling over laughing.

"I know."

After I texted Nolan back, *can't wait*, I looked up to see Jo staring at her own phone.

"What's got your attention like that? You on IG looking at one of those ratchet-ass gender reveal videos? Those things are getting waaay out of hand, if you ask me," I quipped.

Instead of answering me, she tapped the screen of her phone and held it up for me to see. It was a video of my mother wearing heavy eyeliner and smudged orange lipstick, that curly wig she wore on the *Loretha Halter Show* askew on her head, teeth scattered, skin ashen.

Her speech was slurred as she virtually screamed her words. "Yeah, I'm Bridgette Turner's mama. I ain't name her that, but that's what she calling herself now. Y'all think she special 'cause she in a movie? Well, I know the truth about her. She ain't nothing but a broke-down ho', and if y'all wanna hear what I got to say about my so-called daughter, who won't even answer my phone calls and was too damn busy to come to her grandmother's funeral, and ran off the stage of that damn talk show when she saw me, hit up my Cash App. I'm on there as $LetLet. Twenty dollars'll get you the scoop. Loretha Halter ain't tryna pay me, so y'all can get it this way."

The video was posted by *Tea Steepers*, of course, with the caption: *Up and coming actress Bridgette Turner's mom is spilling the tea on her daughter if the price is right and we are here for it!*

I'd seen the clips from after I left the show and saw that my mother had left shortly thereafter, without really sharing anything about me. So I guess I thought I was home free. Now, this.

I sighed and tried not to think about all the hard work I'd put into building my career going down the drain because my mother needed some crack and was willing to ruin my life to get it, handed Jo her phone, and said, "Um, I'm gonna call you later. I know you need to get back home to the girls, and I need to get ready for Nolan. He's on his way home."

"Bridge—"

I stood from the sofa. "Let me walk you out."

Jo sighed. "Okay."

Nolan

I made it home with flowers and Korean takeout in hand, ready to sit down over dinner and let Bridgette talk my ear off if she needed to. And I knew she needed to but didn't want to. She'd avoided it with sex last night, and I knew she'd probably try that again since my weak ass couldn't resist her, because Jo had told me how she was, how she specialized in avoiding the heavy shit. How she could clam up and shut down and wouldn't unlock herself until she was ready. I already knew all of this but had called Jo on my way to work for some advice, because I knew how destructive holding shit in could be. That was Neil's issue. We all knew he and Emery broke up some years back, but he wouldn't share why, and it was obvious that the *why* was eating him up, making him self-destruct. It was hard enough to cope with seeing my twin brother fall apart. I wasn't going to be able to handle watching Bridgette slip away from me. I couldn't lose her to this stuff, so we were going to talk. She was going to talk to me. No sexual distractions.

But then I walked into the kitchen to find her holding two glasses of wine, wearing a damn bra and some panties made out of nothing but silver chains, her nipples peeking at me. Chains. *Chains*, got-dammit!

And well, shit, I couldn't exactly have a coherent conversation with her with my dick as hard as a damn fireplace poker, could I?

*****

You can do this. You can resist her even if you go in that room and she's naked with her ass in the air. So what if your dick gets hard? You don't have to have sex with her.

Yeah, right.

I sighed as I carried the mugs of coffee into the bedroom, damn near dropped them when Bridgette's naked sexy ass yelled, "Damn, baby!"

"What?" I asked, trying to figure out what she was staring at. Couldn't be my dick because it stayed hard and she had to be used to that by now.

"Do you have any idea how fine you are standing there in nothing but those boxers?! Shit! Look at that six pack! Come over here and rub that body on me, Zaddy!"

"Uh, I got coffee."

"And I got some hot chocolate for you." She dug in the bedside table drawer and pulled out a can of Reddi Wip. "With whipped cream." I watched as she opened her legs and covered my favorite place with the whipped cream. "You thirsty?"

When did she take that out of the refrigerator?

My hands shook, and I was about to start spilling coffee

everywhere. I swallowed hard, and said, "We need to talk."

"No, you need to come talk to this pussy."

"N-no, we need to talk about your mother and your feelings about that video. I know you saw—"

"Already handled. I contacted Loretha Halter's producers, got my mother's information, and set up a meeting at the studio office, if that's okay with you. And I want you to be there."

"Y-you're gonna talk to your mother? Really? I just wanted you to talk through your feelings. I didn't expect this, but...I'm proud of you, baby. And yeah, I'll be there with you."

"Good, now you gonna come clean up this mess I made?" She rotated the can in her hand.

I set the coffee on the dresser and licked her dry.

26

Nolan

I think I was more nervous about this meeting than Bridgette as I drove from Malibu to the McClain Films office in Hollywood. A glance to my right gave me a view of a calm Bridgette, pretty as ever, staring out the windshield, but I was so damn wound up, I jumped when my phone started ringing. The screen on the dash told me it was Neil.

"I'll call him back later," I said, more to myself than to Bridgette.

"No, answer it. You have time for a quick conversation with him."

I sighed and answered the call. "Neil, wassup?"

"Damn…you still answering my calls, huh?" he replied.

"Yeah, I told you we're gonna get our shit together. What's on your mind?"

"Um, I need to ask you a favor, and I know what you're thinking. It's not money."

I frowned a little. "Okay, what is it?"

"I been thinking about life and shit, you know? All the stuff I wanted to do, the stuff we used to talk about. Shit, I'm supposed to be scoring your movies right now. You remember that?"

"Yeah, man, I remember."

"We both talked about how we wanted to travel, see the world…I don't know. I see Ev and Leland all happily married, and you got Bridgette. She's a good look for you, a real good look."

I glanced at Bridgette again. She was grinning, her eyes still on the windshield. "Yeah, she is. That's my all, man," I said.

"Man, I'm happy for you. But anyway, I know you wondering why I'm saying all this, so let me get to the point. I want better in my life. I'm tired of being fucked up, and I wanna get myself straight. That's where you come in."

"Okay…"

"There's this rehab program, very exclusive. They don't really fuck with nothing but stars, but I've been researching it, and I think it'd be a good fit for me. It's run by a black actress who was big in the eighties, got an all-black staff, deals with a lot of herbal healing and cleansing and shit."

"Oh, that's right up your alley."

"Right, right. So, I know you the king of connects and I don't wanna bother Ev with this. He's done enough to help me. Shit, more than enough. So, I was wondering if you think you could help me get into this program."

It sounded like it hurt him to ask me for help and that bothered me. What had we become? "Yeah, man, let me look into it, see what I can do."

"Thanks, Nole. I really appreciate it."

"No problem, man."

After I hung up, Bridgette said, "I'm proud of you for helping him."

I shrugged. "He's my brother, my twin. I just wanna see him win."

*****

She wouldn't get out of the car.

The serenity she'd worn on the way to the studio was gone, and now she was sitting in the passenger seat shaking.

"Bridge?" I said softly for the fifth time.

No answer from her.

So I climbed out of my car and walked around to her side. She flinched when I opened the door.

Squatting next to her, I reached up and laid my hand on her thigh. "Bridge, you wanna leave, go back home, cancel the meeting? We can do that if you're not ready for this."

She shook her head. "N-no. I need to get this over with. It's just…I hate this woman, and I hate hating her. I don't think I realized how much I despise her until right now."

"After that shit she pulled in that video, I can't stand her ass, either. We can go if you want to, and I'll understand."

"I…need to do this before she fucks up my career. I just…"

"Hey, look at me."

Her eyes jumped from her hands clasped in her lap to my face.

"You're a lotus, remember? A lotus in full bloom. Beautiful as hell and full of so much damn love that I gotta be the luckiest man on this planet. Whatever she says, whatever she tries to do? It can't change that. You grew out of that mud that she's still stuck in and she wants to dim your light, but she can't, baby. She can't, and she won't."

She stared at me for a moment or two before finally climbing out of my car. Once I was on my feet, she walked into my arms, and whispered, "I love you so much."

"I love you, too, baby."

Bridgette

We met in the conference room, the space where we'd done table reads for *Floetic Lustice*. It was a room with a glass door whose four walls were made entirely of windows, so anyone could see inside of it, but it was a Sunday, so no one was there but us. The long table was sleek and silver; the rolling chairs were padded, comfortable, and a gorgeous shade of teal. This was where I came face to face with my mother for the second time in more than twenty years, if you counted the Loretha Halter ambush.

She was wearing that same wig from the show and the video, but despite it looking dull, it was on her head straight. The orange lipstick wasn't smeared, and someone had applied winged eyeliner and dusty pink eyeshadow to her eyes. She was wearing a red t-shirt with an image of a black woman with an Afro on it. Underneath the Afro woman was the word queen in gold lettering. She also wore a pair of pink, white, and purple patterned leggings with black ballerina flats. She was clean but thin, excruciatingly thin, and I couldn't find even a hint of the pretty woman from my childhood.

The room was quiet as I took her in, almost finding it unbelievable that she'd bullied her way into my world, into the delicately-balanced peace I'd managed to achieve in spite of the horror of my past.

"It's good to see you, Jessie Mae," she said, her mouth spreading into a smile that made me wonder if she'd progressed from crack to meth.

When I didn't respond, Nolan, who was seated next to me, grabbed my hand and squeezed it.

"I saw the video," was how I chose to reply, because I wasn't going to sit there and act like I believed her little happy mother act was real.

"Yeah, I had to do something to get your attention. And it worked."

"So you just wanted to see me? After all these years?"

"I *been* wanting to see you, Jessie Mae. The courts wouldn't let me, and then you ran off here to Hollywood."

"Please stop calling me that."

"It's your name," she said, sounding insulted.

"No, my name is Bridgette Dominique Turner. Wanna see my driver's license? That name you gave me never fit," I gritted.

Nolan squeezed my hand again.

"Why didn't you ever call me back? Why you ain't come to my mama's funeral?"

I bugged my eyes at her. "Are you serious? You actually thought I'd go to her funeral?"

"Yes! That's your family! I don't know what them social workers and shit told you, but blood is blood no matter what! She loved you, talked about how much she missed you all the time. We knew you was out here, because Carmen, Dawnetta's girl, told her mama she'd seen you here. I was glad Dawnetta told me that, because them damn county workers wouldn't tell me shit. And then you started popping up on TV in your expensive clothes talking about this new movie that's coming out. You sitting here next to this man in this suit. I guess you think you better than me now."

"That's why you popped up on the *Loretha Halter Show*? To try to prove I'm not better than you? How did you even get on there?"

She shrugged and scratched at her cheek. "I called that number they put on the screen at the end of the show after they kept advertising that you'd be on there to talk about that movie. I knew it was you even though your name is different, 'cause you look just like you did as a little girl. Tall and skinny, but it look like you done bought you some ass and titties."

"No, I took them after my daddy's side," I said, arching an eyebrow.

"He's dead," she said smugly.

Nolan shifted in his chair.

I assumed that was supposed to hurt me, because she knew I was always crazy about him. But I already knew, thanks to Karen, and had dealt with that grief. "I know," I said.

"Died in the pen. Got shanked," she continued.

"I know that, too. Just like I know you've been in and out of jail for stealing shit and selling pussy."

Her eyes widened and then narrowed. "He wasn't your real daddy, no way. Did you know *that*?"

I couldn't tell if she was lying just to hurt me or if she was telling the truth, and although my heart was stuttering in my chest, I couldn't let her think she'd gotten the best of me. So I said, "Why are we here, Arlette? What did you disrupt my life for? For money? Well, you ain't getting none from me. So you may as well keep posting videos and looking like the desperate crackhead you are."

"I wanna know why you ain't come to my mama's funeral."

"Because I hated her. I *still* hate her. Why else?"

"You still mad about some shit that happened when you was little?"

"You mean her beating me, locking me in closets, and calling me names just for kicks and giggles? Your mother was an evil drug-dealing whore who you let terrorize me for years!"

"You need to let that go. Shit, I had it harder than you when I was growing up!"

"Then why would you want that for me?!" I screamed. Nolan stood from his chair and moved behind me, placing his hands on my shoulders.

"Because I knew it wouldn't kill you. It didn't kill me."

"Yes, it did! You're a fucking career crackhead! You've been a member of the walking dead for years!"

"You ain't no better! You tell this fancy man of yours you was a ho'?" Her eyes rose to Nolan. "She tell you that?!"

"I ain't never been no ho' like you and your damn mother, swapping men and shit! Men in and out of the house screwing both of y'all at the same time while I was locked up in her damn closet and had to hear it. She locked me in there because I wet the bed. I was fucking six! Six and nervous from living in a hell hole!"

"You *were* a ho'! Nothing but a little slut, fucking grown men before your ass was twelve!"

"You let that happen to me! If you'd been half a mother, you would've protected me! But you were too busy tricking for crack, weren't you?! You were never a mother to me!"

She hopped up from her seat and slammed the palm of her hand on the table. "You tell your man about that baby your ho' ass had? Huh? You tell Mr. Money Bags about that, Miss Better-than-everybody-else?!"

After the words left her mouth, the room began to spin, the air became shallow, and my heart raced in my chest to the point that I began to feel light-headed.

Then everything went black.

27

Nolan

Bridgette flew across the table and was on her mother so fast, I didn't have time to react to the whole baby revelation. She was making sounds that weren't in the same stratosphere as any English-language word I'd ever heard, her long, graceful fingers clutching her mother's neck. I hopped over the damn table, too, grabbing Bridgette from behind, but to be so damn thin, my woman was strong as hell and had a death grip—no pun intended—on her mother.

I pulled and tugged and begged Bridgette to let go, because yeah, I knew people who could make the body disappear—like I said, I had the connects—but I didn't want Bridgette to have to deal with the mental strife of having killed her own mother.

"Baby, please let go!" I shouted, and felt her almost release her hold, then it hit me. Like I couldn't resist her pussy, she couldn't resist my commands. So I put a little more bass in my voice, just how she liked it, and said, "Bridgette, let her go! Now!"

Her hands fell to her sides so quickly, I almost thought I dreamed the shit. Her mother grabbed her own neck and fell against the window wall, gasping for air while Bridgette stood there and stared at her. Then Bridgette turned and looked at me, eyes full of tears.

I grabbed her, pulled her to me, and whispered, "It's okay, baby. I got you. I got you." Fixing my eyes on her mother, who at that point, I wanted to fucking strangle myself, I said, "You can go now."

"She tried to kill me! I'm calling the police!"

Bridgette was so out of it, I don't think she heard that bullshit, which was a good thing. So I led her to the nearest chair, sat her down, kissed her forehead, and told her I'd be right back. Then I took her mother at the elbow and led her out of the room.

"Get your hands off me!" she screamed.

I let her go, then got in her face, and said, "Take your ass back to Alabama or wherever you came from and don't look back. No more videos, no more phone calls, no more popping up on talk shows. Stay away from Bridgette."

"Jessie Mae!"

"I don't give a fuck if she calls herself Sideshow Bob. That's what I'ma call her, too, not no Jessie Mae."

"I ain't going nowhere until she pays me! She got all this money now, and she's gonna share! If it wasn't for me, she wouldn't even be here! And I had such a hard time having her, they took my stuff out of me and I couldn't never have no more kids. I am her mother and she supposed to take care of me!"

"Having a baby doesn't make you a mother."

"She knows that better than me. Ask her."

Scratching my forehead and rubbing my hand down my face, I said, "So all of this, you disrupting her life, is about money, not about your mother's funeral?"

"It's about both!"

I shook my head and wanted to put my fist through a wall since I didn't, *couldn't*, hit women. "I'll get you your money."

"Mm-hmm, I knew you was rich. I want—"

"You're gonna take what I give you and sign an agreement to leave her the fuck alone, or I will ruin what's left of your pathetic life, and I mean that shit."

"I don't want nothing to do with her ass, no way. Like I said, she ain't nobody. Just give me the money, and don't be threatening me. You don't know me!"

"And you sure as hell don't know me or what I'm capable of."

She rolled her eyes. "You ain't gon' do shit."

"Keep believing that—you know what? I don't have time for this. You can go now. I'll be in touch."

"You better be."

I watched her leave, then returned to Bridgette to find her with her head resting on the table and tears streaming from her eyes.

*****

Stepping into the foyer of my house, I eased the front door shut and made my way to the kitchen, placing the two containers of breakfast on the counter and then heading to my bedroom, freezing in the doorway at the sight of the empty bed. She was asleep when I left that morning, had climbed into bed and drifted off shortly after we made it home, didn't even eat dinner. I peeked in the bathroom to find that she wasn't in there either. I searched the entire house—no Bridgette. Her car was in the driveway, so she couldn't have gone far.

For some reason, I went back to the bedroom, and just as I was about to pull out my phone to call her, I glanced out the bedroom window and spotted her sitting on the beach, facing the ocean. It looked like she had on one of my t-shirts, and when I got closer to her, I saw that she had on a pair of my jogging pants, too. Without a word, I sat down next to her and placed a hand on her thigh.

With her eyes still on the ocean, she asked, "You're sitting in this sand in your nice white pants?"

I shrugged. "It's just clothes. I don't know if you noticed, but I have a lot more where these came from."

She chuckled. "Yeah, you got more clothes than me, and that's saying something." Her face was wet when she turned to look at me. "I can't stop crying."

"Maybe you need to cry. I read somewhere that it's good for you. It releases toxins or some shit like that."

She nodded and wiped her cheeks. "Where'd you go? Why didn't you wake me up before you left?"

"You needed the rest, and I just had some business to take care of.

Had to meet up with the club's assistant manager since I haven't been able to spend as much time as I want to there lately. Got us some breakfast, too."

"Oh...thank you."

"You're always welcome, baby."

"And you can call the assistant manager Jesse. It doesn't bother me anymore. The first few times I heard you say it, it came on the heels of my mother first trying to contact me, and it was just...a lot."

"Okay. Hey, I saw that post you put on IG."

"Yeah, I'd seen a lot of people wondering about what happened on the *Loretha Halter Show,* and quite a few of them seemed genuinely concerned. So I thought I'd let them know I didn't sign on to air my family issues on TV, but that I was okay."

"I'm glad you did, but it could've waited."

She shrugged. "Um, Nole, I...I don't ever want to see my moth—*her* again. I lost control, and I didn't like how that felt. She just...she brings out the worst in me."

"I don't want you to see her again, either, and I promise she won't bother you anymore."

Her eyes brightened and then narrowed. "What'd you do? You know an assassin or something?"

"I actually do, but I didn't do anything that drastic. I just took care of things. I'ma always take care of things when it comes to you."

"Thank you, I think."

I laughed. "No problem, baby. Oh, and you can expect an on-air apology from Loretha Halter in the next few days."

"Damn, you really don't play, do you? At least you didn't get her fired."

"Only because it seemed to bother you that I got Mike and Rourke fired."

"Well, thank you for that, too."

"I got you, Bridge. Always."

"I'm thankful for that. Um, I think I'm going to call my old therapist. I need to work through this in a healthy way, and I don't wanna burden you with it."

"Okay. Whatever you need."

"And I wanna show you something," she said, grabbing her phone from her lap, swiping and tapping on it, then handing it to me. It was an Instagram account for a young girl named Stacy Bradshaw. She looked to be in her late teens or early twenties, and her profile was full of smiling pictures of her—in a high school cheerleading uniform, in a Crimson Tide sweatshirt, in a unicorn onesie. Some were of her alone, others with friends and family. She was beautiful, tall, and thin, just like Bridgette.

As I stared at the phone, Bridgette said, "I was nine when I was first taken from my mother and put in a series of foster homes after she and her mother were arrested for drug possession. My father was already in jail by then, and my uncle was overseas in the service, so he couldn't take me, not that I think he would've wanted to. He was never close to his mother and sister—my grandmother and mother. Anyway, I was allowed to move back home with my mother when I was ten after she went to rehab and got her own place, and the damn foster homes were so bad, I was actually glad to go back to her. Then she moved back in with her mother about five months later. I stayed with her almost two years before the sorry-ass case worker finally realized I was back in that house with those men coming in and out—crackheads, random niggas off the street, any and everybody. My grandmother's house was always a flop house. But by then, I was already pregnant. I was twelve, and the man who got me pregnant was in his thirties. He was once my grandmother's man. He was nice to me, was always giving me things, and when he started touching me, I just went along with it because he told me it was okay and there was no one in my life to tell me otherwise. He said I was his girlfriend and that he loved me, and I thought that was cool, so I just did whatever he said. Anyway, when I ended up pregnant, my grandmother started talking about how she'd been dreaming about catfish and that she should've known I'd turn out to be a whore. That word? The way she said it? It did something to me, made me feel like I did something bad, like me being pregnant was all my fault. It took a long time for me to understand that I was the victim, that I should've been protected from that. They were in the house when it happened, every time it happened, and I believe they knew. I'm pretty sure he paid my grandmother for me, knowing her."

I swear I wanted to dig her grandmother up and kick her ass. "This is the baby? This is your daughter?" I asked. "Does Jo know about her? Were you gonna tell me about her?"

"Jo knows about everything, except the Lazarus Holmes thing. Haven't gotten around to telling her that yet, and I was gonna tell you. I just…I wasn't ready."

I nodded and set the phone down, giving her my attention.

"I gave her up at birth," she continued. "It was a closed adoption, but I had a…a friend who worked for the state and she was able to track her down for me. I've never contacted her, but I keep up with her through social media."

"It looks like she's happy."

"I believe she is. I believe I did the right thing by giving her up. I have no regrets about that. I mean, I was twelve and living in a youth home. How could I have taken care of her?"

"Is she why you don't want kids…anymore kids?"

She sighed. "I'm not gonna lie and say that wasn't a traumatic experience, having a baby at that age, but truthfully, being a mother has just never been in my plans, like I said before. I wanna conquer this acting world, travel, be free, and love you. That's it. You still okay with that?"

"Yeah, baby. I already told you I'm good with it. I just want you to be okay. That's all I care about."

"I'm gonna be okay as long as you never stop loving me."

"I can't. You're in my soul now. You're a part of me. I'll love you until the day I die, and then my damn ghost will love you."

She smiled and leaned in to kiss me. "I do think I got the best McClain man."

"And I got the best Bridgette Turner. Hey, let's be lazy and spend the day in bed. I can order some food, we can watch some movies, or we can make a movie…"

"Okay, just a second." She took her phone from my lap and I

watched as she texted Jo:

Nolan knows and he still loves me. I am so damn lucky. So blessed.

28

Bridgette

"We in here!" I yelled, after Black, one of Jo's and South's newer bodyguards, opened the door for us. "This better be good, because I'm supposed to be learning lines for my next project *and* I'm missing a *Swamp Murders* marathon."

"Thank God," Nolan mumbled.

"I heard that," I said.

"You heard what, baby?"

Once we made it into the living room, I stopped in my tracks. Jo, who had packed forty pounds onto her tiny frame during her pregnancy with Lena, was wearing a tight little black dress, looking too cute. "Dang, bish! Little Lena done sucked you into a mean-ass snap-back! Oops, where's Nat?"

"In bed. You know it's past her bedtime," Jo responded. "And before you ask, Lena is upstairs with Ms. Sherry. I swear all you care about is my kids. Just…fuck *me*."

"True," I said.

Jo rolled her eyes.

Nolan stepped from behind me and bent down to give Jo, who was sitting on the sofa, a hug. "Hey, sis-in-law."

"Hey, Nolan. I don't know what you see in this woman."

"Shit, me either," Nolan said.

I tilted my head and lifted a brow. "I'ma remember you said that later on."

"Aw, baby. You know I'm playing."

"Mm-hmm."

"Hey, Jo…where's Ev?" Nolan asked.

"Right here," South replied, walking into the room with Neil right behind him.

As Nolan, South, and Neil slapped hands and pulled each other into hugs—damn they were all fine, and since South had made Neil trim that wild-ass beard of his, he and Nolan really looked identical—I turned to Jo, and said, "Guess what we brought to this little shindig?" as the doorbell rang.

Before Jo could respond, Nolan said, "Pineapple vodka."

"Oh, *hell* yeah!" That was Leland, walking into the room with his arm around his wife's waist. She was so pretty to me, and that skin of hers was gorgeous! And unlike mine, her body made sense. Shit, she had curves everywhere. And that baby boy on her hip? I could just eat his little cheeks!

"I didn't know you were gonna be here, man!" Nolan said, as he and Leland gave each other dap.

"Shit, Papa Ev said to be here, so I'm here. Plus, the season is over, so we been out here for a minute. You'd know that, but your ass be up under your woman all the time."

"I know you ain't talking. And have you forgotten that I'm running a film studio, got a film in theaters right now that I'm pushing, and I manage your damn club on top of trying to keep up with this woman here?" Nolan said, as he moved behind me and wrapped his arms around my waist. I tilted my head back so that he could kiss my neck.

"Oh, y'all are so cute!" Kim gushed, as she fell onto the sofa next to Jo who quickly grabbed Little Leland—who wasn't so little anymore—and pulled him into her lap.

"Yeah, they cute, but do you know she taller than you, Nole?" Leland teased.

Nolan spun me around and tucked his bottom lip between his teeth. "Hell. Yeah."

"This nigga must love that shit the way he looking like he about to pounce on her," South quipped.

"I sure do. The higher the heels, the better. Shit, I bought the ones she's got on now," Nolan informed him.

"He really did," I agreed. "And this skirt. He done bought me like a hundred short-ass pencil skirts."

"That's like Leland and waist beads," Kim chimed in. "I have a whole collection of them now."

"Waist beads?" Jo and I asked in unison.

"I told you about pineapples, and you holding out on these waist beads, Leland? That's fucked up!" South said.

"I have arrived!" was how the only McClain sister, Kat, made her entry, followed by Tommy, and Tree, who were both on Leland's security team. That huge living room was filling up for the surprise announcement Jo and South were going to make.

"Damn, about time! What took you so long to get in here? We got here at the same time!" Leland asked Kat.

"I had to fix my makeup. And now I need to use the bathroom. Don't be tryna track me, little brother," she said.

"I'm also your boss, Kit-Kat. Don't forget that!" Leland called after her as she walked away.

"Yeah, yeah, yeah…"

A few minutes later, Sage arrived looking cute in an orange jumpsuit that fit her curves like a second skin, and then South asked everyone to have a seat.

"A'ight, I know y'all all busy with your lives and shit, so I appreciate you for coming over so me and Jo can share this news with you," he began.

"You're having another baby?!" Sage screamed, making Little Leland, who was asleep in his father's lap now, flinch.

"Hell, no!" Jo and South both yelled.

"Oh," Sage said, her voice at a normal volume.

"So, y'all know I been begging Jo to get in the studio with me for a while now, right? Well, she finally broke weak a few months back, and I want y'all to be the first to hear the little EP we made together while she was pregnant. It's just five songs, but they're all bops."

"You let her eat in your studio?" I asked, and everyone laughed.

"Yeah, her little ass was spilling crumbs everywhere," South said through a chuckle.

"Hey!" Jo shrieked.

"I'm just playing, baby," South stated, then lowered his voice, and added, "but not really."

Jo hopped up from the sofa and walked over to him, playfully punching his arm. In response, he pulled her to him, and said, "So anyway, this is a listening party for the *Mrs. South* EP. Here we go." He pressed a button on a remote, and music began pouring from the Beats by Dre-caliber speakers of their stereo system.

Three of the songs were heavily Big South songs with Jo singing soulful, catchy hooks. But on the last two, their roles reversed, with Jo singing the verses and South rapping the choruses. They were all love songs—well, a couple were freaky in nature—and as they played, South explained that he and Jo wrote the lyrics and Neil wrote the music. *Neil. Neil McClain.* Wow! My goodness! Every song sounded so good! This EP was crazy!

After the last track ended, we all applauded and congratulated them. Then Kim yelled, "Hey, play it again!" And once South restarted the EP, she turned to Leland. "Go lay Junior down, baby. I wanna dance."

Looking like he was going to drool at the mere thought of dancing with his wife, Leland left the room with his son on his shoulder. A few minutes later, all of us—with the exception of Neil who just spectated with a smile on his face—were up on our feet dancing to the music, a good mix of up-tempo, mid-tempo, and slow songs. I thought I could get ratchet on the dance floor, but that Kim was a mess! She was rubbing her ass all over Leland, and from the look on his face, he was loving it. Nolan had a hold of me from the back and was grinding on my booty to a nasty-ass song called *Panty Gag* in which Jo sang: "You get so loud, gotta muzzle your mouth. I take my panties off so I can silence Big South." Yeah, South and Jo were freaky as hell.

I watched as Leland whispered something in Kim's ear, and then the two of them snuck out of the living room. I figured they were going to find somewhere to sneak in some sex because this EP was definitely an aphrodisiac. Hell, I was about ready to attack Nolan because of it.

"I wonder where those two are going?" Nolan said into my ear.

"Probably to get in a quickie."

"Huh?"

"I'll explain what that is later, baby."

"What the fuck?!"

The music stopped, and since this was a room full of black people, we all ran in the direction of Leland's voice to find Kat with her legs around Tommy's waist while he had her pinned to the wall just outside the living room.

Nolan

"What the hell is going on?! Everett yelled.

I was too damn shocked to say anything.

"Tommy, are you fucking my sister in my damn house?!" Everett continued.

"Uh, no?" the giant bodyguard replied. "We were just kissing."

"You kissing my sister in my brother's house?!" Leland yelled. "I ain't paying you to kiss my sister!"

"Well, technically, *I'm* paying him. He's just on loan to you," Everett said.

"He's kissing me because I want him to kiss me because he's my man!" Kat said. Then she looked at Tommy. "Put me down, baby."

"Oh, right," Tommy said.

"What?!" Leland, Everett, and Neil all yelled.

I was so relieved that his big ass had moved on, I didn't say shit. I was uncomfortable as hell around him since me and Bridgette got together, even though he'd never said anything to me. But you just never know.

Well, now I knew, and to be honest, Kat looked happier than I'd seen her look in years.

"So y'all been messing around behind my back?!" Leland asked.

Now on her feet, Kat straightened her skirt, and said, "First of all, we are both growner than your ass, so shut up. Second, you can't talk with a stepson that's damn near your age. No offense, Kim."

"None taken. Leland is tripping," Kim replied.

"What?!" Leland said, looking at his wife like she had just spoken in Cantonese or something.

"*And*, we're in love, and I'm...pregnant," Kat announced. "Me and Tommy are having a baby."

I swear everyone in the room shouted, "What?!"

"Are you even divorced yet?!" Neil asked. "I mean, is your divorce final?"

"Yes. It's final, Neil," she said.

She didn't say how long it'd been final, and I didn't want to know.

"Well, congratulations," Jo said, moving to hug Kat, followed by Bridgette and Kim. When I hugged her, Everett gave me a look and I shrugged.

"Yeah, congrats, you two. I'm so happy for you both," Bridgette said. She didn't hug Tommy, and I appreciated that.

"Look," I said. "I get it. You can't control how or when you fall in love. I'm happy for you, sis."

"Man..." Everett shook his head.

"Man, nothing. You need to get over yourself, because we're also getting married. That's why we were kissing." She held out her left hand. "He just proposed, and I said yes!"

Leland's and Everett's heads snapped toward Tommy who shrugged. "It was that music. I was gonna wait to ask her in a few weeks, but I couldn't. I had to do it tonight."

"Got damn," Leland said.

I don't know what hit my ass, but before I realized what I was doing, I had grabbed Bridgette's arm and spun her around from admiring Kat's ring, fell on one knee, and asked, "Will you marry me, Bridgette Dominique Turner?"

"What?!" Jo squealed.

"OMG!" Sage screamed.

"What in the shit is going on here?" Everett mumbled.

"Damn," was Leland's contribution.

"Okay, I see you, Nole!" Neil shouted.

Bridgette gazed down at me, her eyes glistening with tears, and nodded. "Hell, yes!"

"Uh, I'm ordained. I can marry any of y'all," Tree, who lived up to his name, said.

I hadn't even realized he and Black had followed us out into the hallway. "Huh?" I said.

"I'm an ordained minister," he explained. "Got ordained here in California before I moved to St. Louis. I used to preach all the time. Taking a little hiatus right now, but I can marry y'all right now if you want. Y'all can just get the license tomorrow and I'll sign it."

"Can you marry us, too?" Tommy asked.

"Really, baby?!" Kat chirped.

In response, Tommy smiled down at her. "Yeah, let's do it." Damn, he was tall, taller than Kat, and she was taller than me!

I turned to Bridgette, but before I could ask, she said, "Yes. I wanna do it right now.

"What the fuck is happening?" Everett grumbled.

So, there in my big brother's living room, me and Bridgette and Tommy and Kat had a double wedding with Bridgette's friend, Sage, crying through the whole thing. Jo lent us one of her rings that Everett had given her, but I ran out and bought us both rings the next day. And our wedding night? Shit, I hit an all-time low of twenty minutes.

29

Bridgette

"Jo, are you on here?" Sage asked, after she connected all three of us.

"Yeah, what's going on? Bridgette, you on here, too?"

"Yeah, I'm here, and I have no idea what this is about."

It was a little after seven in the morning, I had to be on set for my new movie that afternoon, and my heart was thumping in my chest because Sage had called me crying, saying there was something she needed to tell me and Jo. Shit, was she dying or something?

"Um, I know it's early, but I finally got up the nerve to share this with y'all, and I think I can do it without crying," Sage said.

I doubted that, because her voice was breaking.

"Okay…" Jo said.

"Um, I just wanted you guys to know how much I love you both and how thankful I am that we've been friends all these years. You remember when we first met, Bridge?"

Oh, shit. She *was* dying. Since I was a damn spontaneous crier now, I blinked back tears, and said, "Yeah. We were both at that little club in West Hollywood for that comedy show."

"Yeah, and both of us got there so late there were no tables left and we had to sit at the bar. I was too damn short to climb on the bar stool, and you helped me. Then we both got drunk and shared a taxi ride home," Sage added to the story.

"But you left your purse in the cab and I brought it to you. You were still living with your parents back then and you were doing your sister's makeup the day I brought your purse to you, and I was like, this girl has skills!"

"That was what? Ten years ago?"

"Yep."

"And you introduced me to Jo, and you two let me join your little circle."

"Best decision we ever made," Jo interjected, her voice in shambles from crying now. "What is it, Sage? Whatever it is, we'll help you through it."

"Yeah, we got you," I agreed.

"But there's nothing you two can do about this. There's no hope. There's no hope..." she sobbed into the phone.

"Oh, Jesus! Is it cancer?!" I wailed.

"It's not, is it? Please tell me it's not!" Jo screamed. Then I could hear South's voice in the background, asking what was wrong with her.

"What's going on? You okay? You sound upset? Is that your mother? Give me that got-damn phone!" Nolan had appeared in the living room out of nowhere. I'd left him asleep in bed, but I must've awakened him judging from the grogginess in his voice. Still, I had to tell my coochie to calm down, because it was doing back flips in response to him demanding me to give him the phone. Damn, that turned me on.

"It's Sage, Nole," I informed him.

"Oh, okay," he said, and walked off.

"No! No, I don't have cancer!" Sage yelled into the phone.

"Well, what is it? Diabetes, high blood pressure—oh, shit. Is your ass pregnant?" I asked.

"You don't have AIDS, do you?" Jo queried.

"I'm getting deported!" Sage said.

I frowned. "What? Deported to where? New Jersey? Isn't that where you're from?"

"Hooker, you know I was born in Liberia. We moved to Jersey when I was like two and out here to California when I was ten."

"Oh, shit. That's right! Well, hell...you don't act Liberian, so I forgot," I said.

"How do Liberians act, Bridgette?" Jo asked.

"I don't know, and don't act like you didn't forget she was born there, too."

"Shut up," Jo shot at me. "Wait, you never became a citizen in all these years? You're twenty-nine, Sage. You've been here damn near all your life!"

"It's not that simple. My family came here under temporary protected status because of the war in Liberia, but being here all these years under that protection doesn't automatically qualify you for citizenship."

I leaned forward, feeling relieved that my friend wasn't sick but now worried about her having to leave the country. "But isn't there some way for you to become a citizen or get a green card or something?"

"Well, I don't qualify for employee sponsorship, because I'm self-employed. I don't have a relative who can sponsor me, because my sister married a Canadian and lives in Canada now."

"What are your parents going to do? Do they have a solution for this?" Jo asked.

Sage sighed. "They've decided to go back to Liberia. They say it's their home anyway. But...that's not my home. I don't remember anything about it. I can't go back there!"

"Well, shit, marry Gavin!" I suggested.

"Yeah!" Jo agreed.

"Don't you think I tried that? He won't! He won't marry me and he...he broke up with me. He left last night. That was my only hope. What am I gonna do?" She was crying hysterically now.

"We're gonna fight. We're gonna get you a good lawyer and fight this, you hear me? You are not going anywhere," Jo said.

I backed Jo up with, "That's right. You ain't going no damn where!"

"I don't know...what if—" Sage began, through a sniffle.

"No!" Jo interrupted her. "No 'what ifs.' You're staying in this country with us. You hear me?"

"Yes, I hear you."

All I could do was hold the phone and hope that Jo was right.

Nolan

"You will never know how much I appreciate this, Nole. I mean it. I know I've fucked up a lot over the years, but I'm ready now. I'm ready to get my shit together. I promise you that."

I turned to my brother, my twin, my mirror image, and smiled. "I believe you, man. I don't know why, but I do."

Neil chuckled. "Okay, I guess I deserve that. Hey...congrats again, man. Bridgette is a winner. You got you a good one."

"Yeah, it's been three weeks and I still can't believe she married me. The shit is mind-boggling."

"I was thinking the same thing, but I wasn't gonna say nothing."

"Man, fuck you."

We both laughed, then Neil said, "Damn, it's good to be able to clown with you again and us not be ready to kill each other."

"Yeah, I don't know how things got so messed up between us, but I'm glad we straightened everything out. Hey, if you need anything while you're in there, you can call me. Anytime, day or night."

He dropped his head, staring at the backpack sitting on the floorboard of my car between his legs. "I won't. I gotta do this on my own, no matter how hard it is. This is on me. Plus, you got me in here, paid for my stay. I can't see bothering you after all that."

"You wouldn't be bothering me, Neil. You're my brother, my damn twin."

He smiled at me and nodded. "'Preciate it, Nole. Well, I better get on in there. Thanks, again."

"No problem."

I sat in my car and watched as Neil walked up to the front door of the huge white house with the sign outside it that read *Sankofa Holistic Healing Center*, and after he walked through the front doors, I drove home to my wife.

30

Bridgette

"You sure you're ready to talk to her?" Nolan asked, his hand on my knee.

"Not really, but I know I need to. Got to get some things off my chest."

"All right, let's go."

As he reached for the door handle on the car, I said, "No, I need to go alone."

He dropped his hand and looked at me with a furrowed brow. "You sure, baby?"

"Yeah, I'll be fine."

He kept his eyes on me for a beat or two, leaned in to kiss my cheek, and then nodded.

Taking a deep breath, I climbed out of the car and bit my bottom lip as I made my way to my destination. Once I arrived, I stood there under the October sun and stared down at the marker.

Jessie Mae Parker
Beloved mother. Beloved by her community.

She was buried next to my grandfather, who OD'd before I was born.

Standing there, I felt nothing. No sorrow, no hate—nothing. I was numb, I guess. Or maybe she just no longer held that power over me, the power to change my mood or ruin my day. Maybe, I was finally free of her.

I sighed as I stared down at the plastic yellow flowers on her grave and began to speak to her, "It's Bridg—Jessie Mae. I just wanted to come and...shit, not pay my respects. You know what? I honestly don't know why I'm here; I just know I needed to come talk to you. I guess what I want you to know is that I'm good. No, I'm *great*. I got a good man, a good life, and I'm happy. You didn't break me. You tried, and I don't know if it was intentional or if maybe someone broke you a long time ago and that's all you knew, but that little cycle stops with me. I'm healthy, and my future is so bright. I'm...I won. You hear me? I. Won."

I was wearing a smile when I made it back to the car.

"You good?" Nolan asked, as I slid back into the passenger seat of our rental car.

"No, baby, I'm great."

*****

"Bridgette?!" the woman who was a couple inches shorter than me shrieked. Then she yanked me into a hug that she quickly released me from. "I'm sorry. I just...wow! You're here? In Alabama?"

"Yeah, I'm here. I wanted to—" I turned to Nolan standing behind me and back to Karen. "Karen Seales, this is Nolan McClain, my husband. Nolan, well...I told you about Karen and why we're here."

"Husband! Wow, it's only been what? Eight or nine months since we last talked? You didn't waste time! Or were you already seeing him?"

"No, we had a quick courtship. That seems to be the trend with his family," I explained.

"Well, nice to meet you, Nolan. Oh! Come in! Come in!"

A few minutes later, Nolan and I sat on Karen's sofa, sipping iced tea while she sat in a recliner with a huge smile on her face.

"I am so glad you dropped by, Bridgette! I have missed talking to you, but I know you well enough to know you'd contact me when you were ready," Karen said.

"Yeah, we were in town, so I decided to take a chance and see if you were home. I guess I missed your husband and kids?" I replied.

"Yeah, they're visiting his mother. I had some paperwork to catch up on for work," she said with a wink.

"You're still working for the state, right?"

"Yep. Still doing what I can."

"I'm sure you're doing more than your share. I know you did for me, and that's why I'm here. I want to thank you and to apologize for how I last spoke to you. You've been a good friend to me, and you didn't deserve that. You went above and beyond for me, and I just want you to know that I truly appreciate you. I am so sorry for the things I said."

"No, no, I was wrong to give your moth—Arlette your number. But when I saw the obituary in the paper, I called and told her I was a friend of yours and she sounded so pitiful. I just...I thought giving your number to her was the right thing to do, but it wasn't. I should've let you contact her when you were ready."

I nodded. "Uh, Stacy graduated."

"I know, and she got a scholarship to 'Bama."

"Yeah, I saw that. I'm proud of her."

"She's a smart girl, just like you. I hope you two get to meet one day."

"If she ever reaches out to me, I won't reject her."

"I know you won't. Oh! Did you hear that Arlette is in jail?

My mouth dropped open. "Again? For what?"

Karen shrugged. "I don't know. She was arrested in California. That's all I heard."

About thirty minutes later, once we were back in the rental car on our way to the airport, I asked Nolan, "Did you have my mother arrested for something?"

"If I did, I wouldn't tell you."

I shook my head as I gazed out the window. Nolan and his damn connections.

31

Bridgette

We were in Costa Rica, a surprise little weekend getaway delayed-honeymoon Nolan planned for us during a break in my filming schedule. Our bungalow was right on the beach, mere inches from the ocean, and as I stood on the balcony, I couldn't tear my eyes away from the beautiful sunset.

His hands were the first thing I felt—warm, strong, encasing my upper arms. Then his lips on the back of my neck, his erection on my butt. He was naked, but shit, so was I.

Without uttering a word, he eased a hand around my body to my center and gripped my sex. I widened my stance and leaned over the banister with a moan as he played with me, his tongue blazing a trail down my back.

"You are so wet. Is that for me, baby?" he asked.

"Mm-hmm," I hummed.

When he entered me, I gasped and gripped the wooden banister, my breasts dangling, my whimper being drowned out by the crashing waves. Nolan gripped my hips, sliding in and out of me with ease, smacking my ass, kissing my back, making me want to crawl out of my skin and into his. Damn, he felt good!

His body began to crowd mine as his warm breath hit my ear. "I love you, baby," he whispered, still massaging my yoni stroke by stroke, diving deeper and deeper inside of me. "I love you so much."

"I...love...you...tooooo!"

We made love until the sun was hidden beneath the ocean, until we were both drenched in sweat, until we were so exhausted we fell into bed without eating dinner.

Nolan

"Is that your phone?" Bridgette's voice sounded so damn fuzzy and distant, I first thought I'd imagined it. Then I realized the haze of sleep was making me think that.

"What?" I asked, my face still buried in the pillow.

"That's gotta be your phone. I turned mine off."

That's when I heard the outlying ringing of a cell phone and remembered leaving mine in the bathroom. "They can leave a message."

"It might be important, Nole."

"Shit, Bridge. I was sleeping good."

"Well, you're up now. May as well answer it."

Groaning, I stumbled out of bed but had missed the call by the time I got to the phone. Dragging myself back to the bed, I muttered, "It was Uncle Lee Chester."

"Call him back."

"Bridge, come on. It's too damn early."

"Something could be wrong with one of your aunts or something. Call him back."

"If that was the case, he'd call Ev or Leland. He probably don't even want nothing."

"You won't know that for sure if you don't call him back, Nole."

"Fine. I'll call him back. Shit!" I tapped his number on the screen, put it on speakerphone, laid the phone on my stomach, and closed my eyes.

"Nolan! What-up-there-now?!"

"Hey, Unc…you called?"

"Yeah, yeah. I know you down in Costa Reefer on your honeymoon, but I heard something I wanted to tell you. It's important."

"Okay?"

"Earl was telling me about this song. It say something about eating groceries on your woman's booty. I thought you should know that since y'all honeymooning and shit."

Bridgette's ass jumped up and ran into the bathroom laughing.

"Uh, Unc—"

"I don't know what kind of groceries, but probably just, you know, some crackers, chocolate chip cookies, a slice of cheese, some ham loaf, maybe a piece of pound cake. You know…groceries!"

"Unc—"

"Yeah, you supposed to put the groceries on her ass, or maybe in her ass. Naw, that shit don't sound right."

"Unc, I got it! I got it!"

"All right, good. Tell Bridgette I said hi. What time is it over there anyway?"

"We're just an hour behind y'all in Texas."

"Shit, it's still early then. I'll let you go."

"Bye, Unc." I ended the call and looked up to see Bridgette standing at the end of the canopy bed with a big-ass grin on her face, looking beautiful in the early morning light. "I told you he didn't want shit."

"No, he gave you some valuable information."

"Bring your valuable information ass here."

She got that look in her eyes that she always got when I told her to do something, crawled into the bed, straddled me, and said, "Yes, sir?"

I smacked both her thighs and watched as her eyes flashed with what I knew was desire.

"What was that for?" she asked.

"That's Nolanese for, 'Thank you for being my wife.'"

"Ohhh…" She leaned forward and kissed me. "You're more than welcome, baby."

A southern girl at heart, Alexandria House has an affinity for a good banana pudding, Neo Soul music, and tall black men in suits. When this fashionista is not shopping, she's writing steamy stories about real black love.

Connect with Alexandria!
Email: msalexhouse@gmail.com
Website: http://www.msalexhouse.com/
Newsletter: http://eepurl.com/cOUVg5
Blog: http://msalexhouse.blogspot.com/
Facebook: Alexandria House
Instagram: @msalexhouse
Twitter: @mzalexhouse

Also by Alexandria House:

The McClain Brothers Series:
Let Me Love You
Let Me Hold You
Let Me Show You

The Strickland Sisters Series:
Stay with Me
Believe in Me
Be with Me

The Love After Series:
Higher Love
Made to Love
Real Love

Short Stories:
Merry Christmas, Baby
Baby, Be Mine

Text alexhouse to 555888 to be notified of new releases!

Made in the USA
Las Vegas, NV
21 November 2024

12308641R00114